HAUNTED AND HEXED

BLACKWOOD BAY WITCHES COZY MYSTERY BOOK 1

MISTY BANE

Haunted And Hexed © 2019 Misty Bane

Cover design by Molly Burton at Coverworks

CHAPTER 1

*W*hen you have two cars stolen from you within forty-eight hours and end up stranded on the side of the road in the third, you start to consider that the universe doesn't want you to get where you're going.

"Need a hand?" he called out through his passenger side window.

I really wasn't much for surrendering to the whole damsel-in-distress thing, but here we were. Typically, I would roll my eyes and wave him on with something like, *"Thanks, but my big, strong cop/biker/boxing champion of the world boyfriend will be here any minute."* But at that moment, I decided to weigh this man's offer a bit more carefully. I was just two miles shy of my destination and I'd even considered giving up and walking, but literally everything I owned was in the backseat of the rental car.

In my defense, between driving nonstop for two days, save a few hours of sleep on lumpy beds in cheap hotels, the summer heat, and the emotional rollercoaster I'd been on recently, oh, and the whole car theft thing, I was completely burnt out and on the verge of a breakdown.

Enter my knight in shining armor. He *was* in a police car, after all, so I figured he was probably a safe bet. I took a quick glance at my passenger seat to confirm that my purse—or more specifically, my taser—was within easy reach, and made the snap decision that it was probably in my best interest to forego the independent woman routine for once and just let the guy change my tire. Also, full disclosure, I was just about to use my phone to call for AAA, because I didn't *actually* know how to change a flat.

"That would be great," I said with a smile, but he was already pulling his cruiser over to the side of the road in front of me. He hopped out and I instantly noticed that he was casually dressed in a plain black T-shirt and gray cargo shorts.

"Uh, interesting police uniform," I eyed him.

"Oh, I'm not actually a cop," he said. I imagine he must've seen a look of panic cross my face because he followed up with, "I'm kidding!" He laughed then, exposing a row of perfect white teeth. He was undisputedly handsome in that works-out-seven-days-a-week-and-practices-impeccable-hygiene kind of way.

"Hey, I'm sorry if I scared you." He knitted his brow with concern. "I'm just off-duty. Took my cruiser in for an oil change." He smiled again and knelt next to me in front of the offending tire. I noticed he had a bit of stubble on his face, like he hadn't shaved for a few days, and I saw the black lines of a tattoo peeking out from under the sleeve of his T-shirt. Perhaps he wasn't the pretty boy I'd initially pegged him for. Still, despite how attractive he was, he wasn't really my type. Although, in all honesty, my type, as it turned out, seemed to be

2

the lying, cheating narcissist. Yeah, my man-picker was definitely broken.

He offered his hand, "Wolf Harper."

"Wolf?"

"Yeah, it's a family name. German. Feel free to just call me Harper though. Everyone does." I noticed then that he had the bluest eyes I'd ever seen, and they lit up when he smiled. It gave me that fluttery feeling in my stomach and I didn't like it. In my experience, men who gave you fluttery feelings were always trouble. I was starting to regret not calling AAA and dealing with it myself.

"I'm Dru." I took my sweaty hand back and immediately realized that I must've looked like an absolute mess. I hadn't showered since the day before and losing the air conditioner in my car earlier that morning meant that the makeup I'd carefully applied in my rearview mirror had melted off. I did a quick swipe under each eye for the smeared mascara that must have been there and ran a hand over my hair.

"Dru? Is that a nickname?" he asked.

"Yeah, it's short for Drusilla." I stood and happened to catch him making a strange face. I leaned against the side of my car to watch him work.

"I know. It's very… children's movie villainess. Hence the nickname."

He shook his head, "No, sorry. It's just that I knew a Drusilla. She passed very recently though." He paused to wedge the flat tire from its rim. "Kind of a grumpy old gal." He grunted. "At least that's what she wanted everyone to think, but she was a good lady. Well, as long as she liked you." He chuckled.

"My grandmother," I said. It felt strange saying it. Up until two weeks prior I hadn't even known she existed, and now here

I was moving to her hometown and inheriting everything she owned, including a successful bookstore.

He stopped and looked up at me. "Drusilla was your grandmother?" He looked genuinely surprised.

"You didn't figure it out? I mean, how many Drusillas have you actually met in your life?" I teased.

"Touché," he snickered, "So, you just in town to see the place before you sell it or...?"

I wasn't sure why I felt offended by his question, but I was. "No. I'm here indefinitely."

He perched up onto his tiptoes and gave a quick glance at the inside of my car before he went back to work.

"Didn't bring much," he offered in explanation. That was true. I'd been living with my father for the past two months after a bad breakup. If catching your fiancé cheating with your best friend since childhood counted as 'bad breakup.'

"I brought the most important thing," I said, more to myself than to Harper, reaching inside the open back window to stick my finger into my cat's wire travel carrier. He pawed at it playfully.

"Cute. What's her name?" Harper grunted as he twisted the crowbar to tighten the lug nuts.

"He. This is Maui Lane." I took my hand back.

He smiled. "Cute. Again." He winked up at me.

"I think you mean clever," I said.

"That too." He gave me a quick half smile before his face turned serious again. "Well, I'm really sorry about your grandmother."

"Thanks," I said, though I still felt disaffected. I'd never met her before and I didn't know a single thing about her until a week ago. The loss I felt seemed like it was more for the fact that I'd never have the opportunity to know her now.

4

"Pretty cool you actually showed up."

"How's that?" I asked.

"Well, I mean," he paused and I caught myself watching his biceps as he tightened lug nuts. *Stop it,* I scolded myself. "You never met her, right? So, this woman you don't even know leaves you everything she owns, including a business, in a town you've never even been to, and your first inclination wasn't to just have a real estate agent sell the place for cash. That's what a lot of people would've done."

"How do you know all of that? That I never met her?" I asked.

"I take it you've never lived in a small town before?" He grinned.

I shook my head. I'd grown up in the suburbs, just on the outskirts of Las Vegas. Small town life was completely foreign to me.

"Everyone knows just about everything about everyone else," he continued, "and word travels fast. By the way, I'm sorry if I overstepped."

"No, you didn't," I said. "To be completely honest, curiosity more than anything brought me here." I fidgeted with the amber ring on my middle finger. "I might still sell it eventually. I haven't decided yet. But I wanted to come here first and see this place. Both of my parents were born here and my grandmother spent her whole life here. I might never have had the chance to meet her... but I'm hoping maybe I can learn some things about her from this place." I suddenly felt very uncomfortable. It wasn't in my nature to share so much with a complete stranger. I figured it must've been the heat and possible dehydration getting to me. I crossed my arms over my chest and shuffled my feet a bit.

"I like that." He nodded and gave me a soft smile.

He stood then. "Well, there you go. All fixed up." He grabbed the pathetic flat tire lying on the gravel and threw it into the back of his cruiser. "I'll get this fixed and bring it by the bookstore tomorrow." He turned to me again and smiled. I don't think I'd ever met a man that smiled as much as this one.

"Need directions to your new place or do you know where you're headed?" He ran his hand through his sandy colored hair.

"I think I can manage." I waved my phone.

"Okay. Well, um, the police station is right in the middle of town, just a block down from you, toward the Bay. Let me know if you need anything, okay?"

"Sure. Thanks for your help." I hopped into my rental car and realized he was waiting for me to drive away first so he could follow me into town. What a gentleman, I mused.

No, Dru, he's a cop. Of course, he's going to wait for you to pull away first. That's what they always do. You're being ridiculous. Just stop, I scolded myself again. And yet, I still caught myself staring into my rearview mirror more times than I'd like to admit.

∼

J sat at the single blinking light of an empty intersection, looking back and forth between the paper I'd scribbled the address on and the building itself. What was immediately apparent was what my grandmother's lawyer hadn't mentioned to me: this wasn't your run of the mill bookstore. No, this wasn't a sweet old lady drinking tea all day and helping customers between reading chapters of Agatha Christie books.

What stood in front of me, quite ominously, I might add, was an entirely different beast. It was a three-story building, its chipped white paint showing its age, with sage-colored trim that boasted nearly floor-to-ceiling windows on all sides of the first two stories. The topmost level had a more modest number of windows, some with curtains, and I assumed it was where my grandmother had kept her residence. Fancy-looking wrought-iron letters nailed next to the maroon colored door told me this was it: 777 Hemlock St. There was a modestly-sized plaque the same color as the door and its gold lettering that read: *INVOKE: A Metaphysical Specialty Shop and Bookstore.*

I had no idea what 'metaphysical' even meant, but I had a feeling this was one of those places that smelled of too much incense, where you could buy a bag full of crystals and a book on astral projection. Not knocking anyone's preferred method of spirituality, but it wasn't something I had any experience with. My father had taken me to church some as a kid. Not enough that I actually remembered much of anything, but just enough to ingrain the Catholic guilt.

I pulled up to the curb in front of the bookstore and decided to go in and check things out before I brought in my luggage. The sun was blistering, so I grabbed Maui's travel carrier and brought him with me. The sign on the front door was turned to CLOSED, but I tried the knob anyway. The lawyer had told me that someone would be there to meet me when I arrived, and I was hoping whoever that 'someone' was hadn't forgotten.

Thankfully, the door swung open with ease. It didn't have a bell on it to announce my arrival the way most businesses do, but as soon as I entered a girl popped up from behind the register counter.

I gasped, nearly dropping Maui.

"Sorry if I scared ya!" She giggled. At first glance, I thought she was a young teenager. Two blonde pigtails sat near the nape of her neck and her lipstick was a shade primarily spotted on young girls during their first venture into makeup. She wore a white shirt with a picture of a cat wearing glasses and reading a book on the front. Something you might see in the children's section of your local department store. The bright reddish-pink hue of her lipstick matched the plaid skirt she was wearing. After my initial shock subsided, I realized she was more likely a woman in her early twenties.

"Oh, that's all right. I just startle easy," I joked and shoved the stray hairs back from my face.

She made no attempt to introduce herself.

"So do you work here, or...?" I asked.

"Sure did. Nice to meet you. I'm Beatrix Jane La Mont. But everyone calls me Trixie," she announced, a huge grin plastered on her face as she extended her hand in that awkward way that a child does for a handshake. "Oh, wait. Sorry. Still getting used to this." She giggled.

"Hi." I set Maui's carrier down. "I'm Drusilla—*Dru*—Rathmore Davis. Drusilla Rathmore's granddaughter," I introduced myself. I had been given my mother's maiden name as well as my father's last name.

I looked back up to grab her hand, but she was already running around the counter.

She stopped inches in front of me. "Well, just look at you! Gosh, I'm so sorry! Here I am, waiting for your arrival, and I can't believe I didn't recognize you! You look just like your granny! Oh, I *so* wish I could hug you!" She gave me an ear-piercing squeal.

I should've been offended that she thought I resembled an eighty-year-old woman, but I had a sneaking suspicion that Trixie wasn't exactly winning in the IQ department. She really wasn't making much sense and my head was already pounding from a combination of too much heat, dehydration, and her shrillness.

"And who is this?!" She knelt in front of Maui's carrier. She sort of smelled like cotton candy and, mixed with the overpowering scent of incense running rampant in the store, it was making me a little nauseous.

"Careful," I started, but Maui began to purr. It was odd. He rarely liked anyone, much like his owner.

"Huh, he likes you," I said, more confusion in my voice than I intended. "His name is Maui Lane."

Trixie giggled again. I could tell she was going to drive me absolutely batty. No one should be this chipper. Ever.

I heard the door bang closed behind me and I jumped again. First thing on my list was buying a bell for that door.

"*Helloooo!*" Two voices in perfect unison sang out behind me.

I turned to face two women that must've been about my grandmother's age. I waited for Trixie to address them, but she didn't even look up, seemingly distracted by Maui. *Okay, well, I guess I am the owner now*, I thought.

"Um… sorry. We're closed," I said.

The tall one burst out laughing. "Oh, come here, sweetie." She pulled me in for a hug with a shocking amount of strength. Once she released me, she stood back and let the shorter, plumper one have a go at me.

"We're the welcome wagon!" She announced proudly.

"I'm Dorothy, and this is Minnie." The taller one used her thumb to point at the short woman next to her. Dorothy was probably just shy of six feet, with a head of curly white hair. Minnie was a bit more average in height but she had a matching hairstyle. They both were quite done up in their pantsuits—

Dorothy's a teal color and Minnie's red—and kitten heels, a face full of makeup, and shiny baubles hanging from their ears.

"Well, it's nice to meet you. I take it you knew my grandmother then?" I shuffled my feet, feeling a bit overwhelmed. These new faces were so welcoming, but all I really wanted to do was take a shower and a nap.

"Oh, yes, dear. Since birth. Our mothers were like sisters." Dorothy nodded before turning her attention to a tie-dye curtain covering an opening at the back of the store. As if on cue, a woman emerged. She looked to be about my age, which is twenty-eight, by the way. She was quite voluptuous, highlighting her curves in a sleek black outfit. Her long dark hair bounced when she walked and her whole face seemed to radiate an openness when she smiled.

"I'm so sorry I didn't hear you come in!" She carried an armload of books and set them down on the edge of a long wooden table covered with a wide array of colorful crystals.

She hurried over and wrapped me up in a quick hug.

"I'm Heather." She pulled back to look at me but kept her hands on the back of my arms. "It's so great to meet you! We've all just been so anxiously awaiting your arrival!"

It dawned on me that I had yet to introduce myself to anyone but Trixie, the apparent cat whisperer. "Wait, how do you all know who I am?"

"Ah, magic," Minnie offered, a twinkle in her eye. They all laughed in the way that people do when they share an inside joke, but not a single one answered my question.

"Can I help you bring in your things?" Heather asked.

"Oh, it's fine. I can unload the car myself." I said, but Heather was already on her way out the door.

"Good grief." Dorothy rolled her eyes. "I apologize no one was here to greet you when you first arrived. We would've been here much earlier but we had a bit of an issue with… well, let's just say Minnie isn't allowed to cook alone, yet she takes every opportunity she can to try to prove herself. Much to the chagrin of the rest of us. No one likes cleaning up others' messes." She side-eyed a rosy-cheeked Minnie, who scowled back.

"Oh, no. It's okay, actually—" I started and motioned toward Trixie.

"They can't see me," Trixie said in a casual tone, not looking up from Maui.

"What?" I looked down at her.

"What?" Dorothy repeated.

"Is your cat talking to you?" Minnie snorted.

"No… *what?*" I said again, looking from the confused faces of Minnie and Dorothy back down to Trixie.

"I said they can't see me," Trixie repeated. "I wouldn't mention that you can though. At least not yet." I looked up at Dorothy and Minnie but they both stared at me, Dorothy with an arched eyebrow and Minnie looking utterly confused. I didn't really understand why they were messing with me. I thought hazing ended after college.

"It's nice to have you here." Minnie changed the subject. "Is Drusilla here as well?"

"*I'm* Drusilla. But I strictly go by Dru. I thought you all knew who I was?" I realized I might've been just as confused as Minnie was.

"No, dear, I meant your Granny." Minnie gave me a puzzled look just before Dorothy elbowed her.

"What?" Minnie scowled. I had no idea what was going on here. I had a senile old lady that seemed to have forgotten my grandmother was dead and a girl telling me she's invisible. Things weren't starting out well at all.

"She *just* got here." Dorothy snarled at Minnie before

turning to me, "Sorry, dear. Minnie—just ignore her. Half the
time she doesn't make any sense and the other half she *really*
doesn't make any sense." Dorothy shot Minnie what looked like
a warning, just as Heather came barreling into the store with
half of the contents of my backseat.

"I'll just put this stuff upstairs for you. That's where the
apartment is," she called as she passed. She banged Trixie in the
side of the head with my hard plastic suitcase as she walked by,
but Trixie didn't budge. She just kept right on cooing at Maui.

"Anyway, we just wanted to stop in and say a quick hello.
I'm sure you're quite tired from your trip and in need of fresh-
ening up." *Was it that obvious?* "We best be on our way so you
can get settled," Dorothy said.

"Hello?" I heard a hesitant voice and jumped. I *really*
needed to buy a bell for that door.

Minnie and Dorothy turned, and I was able to see the
woman standing behind them. She was a petite thing wrapped
up in perfectly applied makeup and a gorgeous tan. Her hair was
almost to her waist and so shiny, the light from the windows
bouncing from it effortlessly. It was the same white color as
mine, though hers had that perfect beach wave that could only
be mastered with the perfect genes and the perfect curling iron.
She wore a turquoise sundress and matching heels. I was
instantly aware of my unkempt ponytail, bare face, plain tank
top, and cutoff jean shorts. Even on a really good day, I
would've had the confidence of a middle school girl standing
next to her.

"Yes?" Dorothy spoke. "Didn't you see the CLOSED sign
on the door?" I watched Dorothy size her up and thought I heard
the sound of sirens in the distance.

"Um," she ignored Dorothy's rudeness and made a little
giggling noise as she smiled. "I didn't realize there'd be so

many of you here to greet me. What a welcoming little town. Everyone I've met has been just so nice. You all really know how to make a girl feel at home." She glanced around at each of us and must've caught the resounding look of confusion on our faces. "Oh gosh, sorry. I'm rambling. I tend to do that." She rolled her eyes and adjusted the white designer bag on her shoulder. I'd purchased exactly one white purse in my lifetime and its luster had lasted almost as long as my last blind date.

The young woman extended her hand to Dorothy, but the firetruck and cop car whizzing by outside the window caught Dorothy's attention first.

Dorothy turned to Minnie and whispered, "They must have found the body."

I felt my eyes widen.

The young woman stepped forward now, shoving her hand in front of Dorothy, and I watched a look of agitation pass on her flawlessly painted face.

"Pleased to meet you," she said. "I'm Drusilla Rathmore Davis."

CHAPTER 2

J felt a rush of panic. *A body?* Yes, that's definitely what Dorothy had said, but I'd have to ask about that in a minute because did this woman just say she was me?

"Pardon?" Dorothy put her hand to her chest, taken aback and refusing the handshake.

"Drusilla Rathmore Davis. And who are you?" The woman said more firmly.

"You most certainly are not Drusilla Rathmore Davis." Dorothy challenged her.

Now it was the woman's turn to put a hand to her chest, appearing shocked. "Yes, I am."

"Nope. No way." I heard Heather coming up behind me. She put a hand on my back as she passed and stood next to me.

"What do you mean? What is this?" The woman's eyes narrowed, and she looked at each of us accusatorily. "This is *my* grandmother's store. Who are all of *you*?"

I tried to form words but there was a disconnect from my brain to my mouth.

"No," Heather crossed her arms over her chest, "you're

not." She walked toward Fake-Dru and I thought for a second she might shove her out the front door. Instead, she flipped a white curl off the woman's shoulder.

"First, the hair's all wrong." Heather waved her hand and walked back towards me. She spun me around and yanked my ponytail up to reveal the deep red section of hair just at the nape of my neck. It was an oddity I had been born with and my father had told me once that I should be proud of it, because my mother had it too. One of the many wonderful things I'd inherited from her, he'd said.

"*This* is Rathmore hair. And *this* is Drusilla Rathmore's granddaughter." Heather crossed her arms over her chest again and jutted her hip out as if she'd just won the most difficult case in all of history.

"Well, that's—" Fake-Dru put her hands on her hips. "I dye my hair!" she exclaimed, "The red streak is just ugly. I've been bleaching it out since I was a teenager." Well, that was just rude. She raised her chin a bit. "And she could've easily dyed hers too, trying to mimic Rathmore hair."

"True. But I used to be a hairstylist and I know the white you have there isn't real either. I can see your dark roots." Heather smirked and Fake-Dru looked like she'd been slapped in the face.

There was a weird standoff happening here that I should've been more involved in.

"Maybe there's been some kind of mix-up?" I said weakly. I looked at Dorothy and Minnie. If they'd known my grandmother her whole life, then surely they'd know about her family, I hoped. Dorothy opened her mouth, but Fake-Dru beat her to it.

"This… *person,*" Fake-Dru waved her hand aggressively in my direction, "is obviously trying to pose as me and steal my identity! Let me see your ID." She took a step closer and jabbed her finger at me. "What are you after? My grandmother's store? What's your endgame here, huh?" She looked really angry and, for a second, I forgot that she was the fake one.

"No, look. There's obviously some kind of mix-up here," I stated again, finally finding my voice. "*I'm* Drusilla Rathmore Davis. That doesn't mean you aren't too, okay?

Drusilla Rathmore was my grandmother. Maybe she had two granddaughters who both happen to have the same name? Maybe the lawyer forgot to mention that when he contacted each of us.

Okay, in retrospect, I realize that made no sense. Even if my grandmother had two granddaughters named after her, we wouldn't share the same last name. Unless my dad had somehow dated a woman behind everyone's backs, gotten her pregnant, convinced her to name her child after his late wife's mother, and then never saw either of them again.

Yeah, the logic certainly wasn't there, but the last few days had been rough and the culmination of it all was having its way with me. It was also making me hallucinate because Trixie, the girl who no one else could see apparently, said, "She's upsetting Maui."

"He's fine." I looked down at her.

"What? Who's fine?" Fake-Dru furrowed her brow.

"I told you they can't see me. Can't hear me either, obviously." Trixie rolled her eyes at me.

"Okay, enough with that." To say I was annoyed would've been an understatement.

"No, *you* enough! What are you even doing here?" Fake-Dru narrowed her eyes. "Look, I received a call from my grandmother's lawyer saying that she left this place to me." She jabbed her finger furiously. "I was so excited to come here and meet all the people who knew my grandmother. I never met her and I was so looking forward to learning about her and following in her footsteps by running this store. I've been studying the metaphysical my whole life!" I really needed to look up that word. She gave me a pout. "I had such a great start this morning and now you all are ruining it!"

"Oh, good grief!" Dorothy had one of those voices generally reserved for mothers—the firm, threatening type. "Listen," she grabbed Fake-Dru by the shoulders and turned her around, "you are *not* Drusilla's granddaughter. Everyone in this room knows that. Now I suggest you leave before I get angry."

She had her back to me, but something in Dorothy's eyes must've sold Fake-Dru on the idea, because a wave of fear passed over her face. She composed herself though, flipped her hair back off of her shoulders, and adjusted her bag again. She walked to the door, but turned back just as she opened it.

"This is ludicrous and incredibly upsetting. I'm sure my grandmother is just rolling over in her grave right now. I will be back. And next time, I'll have my grandmother's lawyer and the police with me!" she declared with confidence, but as soon as the words left her mouth she hurried out of the doorway and nearly ran down the sidewalk until she was out of view.

Trixie giggled. "She's lucky Granny isn't here. That old spitfire would've ripped her to shreds." Weird. That was exactly the way my father had described my grandmother too and thoughts of him invaded my mind.

I had been so angry at him when I'd left home. My whole life he had a hard time talking about my mother, and I felt like I knew little more than her name and the things about me that reminded him of her. I didn't even really know how she'd died. An accident, my father would always say. But all of my internet research had proved futile. I'd been an infant at the time, so I never even had any real memories of her.

He never talked about where he'd come from either. I had always assumed I'd been born in the place that I'd grown up in, but when the phone call from my grandmother's lawyer came, my whole world came crashing down with it for the second time in a month.

I'd learned that both of my parents originated from Blackwood Bay and my grandmother had been here my entire life. Someone who could've shared stories about my mother with me, someone I could've bonded with, a mother figure, and I had felt like my father had taken it all away from me and now that she was dead, I'd never have that opportunity back.

I'd cried and yelled but all he did was hang his head and apologize and tell me that we'd left because it hadn't been safe to stay. Fueled by my anger, I'd decided to leave while he was at work. But he was really all I'd ever had. I left a simple note on the kitchen counter:

I'll call you when I'm ready. Still love you, Dad. -Dru

I decided I'd call him the next day just to let him know I'd made it okay.

"Well, that was weird." Heather's voice interrupted my thoughts and she handed me a bottle of water.

"I'll say!" Minnie shook her head in disgust. I set to work chugging the water when a realization hit me. I stopped and a bit of water dribbled down my chin.

"Wait. How do you all know I'm really Drusilla's granddaughter? I mean, the hair isn't really akin to a DNA test or anything."

"Granny," Minnie said.

"Sorry?" I wiped my chin.

"She always went by Granny. Never her full name. The kids around town always called her that—" Dorothy began.

"Because of her white hair," Minnie butted in.

"Right. Anyway, she was a local staple, your grandmother. She used to stand outside the store every day with a basket full of candy waiting for the kids to get out of school. They'd pass by and she'd chat with them for as long as they wanted. They all loved her." Dorothy's eyes started to tear up.

"The older she got, the surlier she became, but she adored those kids. Even after they'd grown they'd always come back and visit her. She sort of adopted every kid in sight and became the token town grandmother." Dorothy wiped under both eyes. "But enough nostalgia for now." She smiled and waved her hand in front of herself. "To answer your question, dear—"

"What was her question?" Minnie interrupted.

"She asked how we knew she is who she says she is." Dorothy gave a gentle smile and I realized that the two of them may very well be sisters.

Dorothy turned back to me and I could see a wave of thoughts passing through her mind. Finally, she said, "We just… we just do."

"Magic!" Minnie proclaimed. A big smile spread across her face and she giggled. Trixie giggled along with her.

"Okay, what do you all see here?" I stood in front of Maui's travel carrier, Trixie's back to me. She didn't seem affected by my question.

"A cat in a cage?" Heather raised her eyebrows. I looked to Dorothy and Minnie. They glanced at each other and then back at me.

Trixie let out an exasperated groan. "I know *you* can hear me, Dru. Do you think I'm lying or something?"

"Are you all right, dear?" Dorothy stepped toward me, her brow knitted with worry.

"Heather," she said, not taking her eyes off of me, "why don't you get Dru upstairs and help her get settled enough to take a nice, long shower and maybe get some rest? I'm sure she's had a long day."

"But—" I started to protest.

"Of course!" Heather jumped forward and put her arm around my shoulders like I was some pitiful creature she was tasked to care for.

"We'll stop back in tomorrow and check on you," Dorothy stated. I guess invitations to visit weren't par for the course around here.

"Come on, sweetie." Heather started to turn me around when I remembered what Dorothy had said earlier.

"Wait!" I spun around, startling all three of them. Trixie remained unfazed, her usual state, it seemed. I looked at Dorothy. "When the firetruck and cop cars drove by earlier, I heard what you said. Something about them finding a body?"

She nodded. *A little more information, lady.*

"How did you know that?" I asked.

She frowned.

"Did someone go missing around here or something? Do you know whose body it was?"

And without missing a beat, Trixie popped up from her spot on the floor. "Mine! Duh!"

"Yes, sadly." All three women looked down, sadness on their faces, and Dorothy spoke for them. "Our sweet Trixie. She worked here along with Heather."

"Is that a joke? What's going on?!" I demanded. I was sick of this bizarre game they were playing with me. My grandmother's friends were either crazy or sadistic, and I was over it.

I looked around at the faces scowling at me, except for Trixie's of course. A wide smile spread across her face. "I told you!" she giggled.

I ignored her. "Can you all stop now please? This isn't funny." I could feel a lump in my throat. *Do not cry*, I willed myself. I was not a crier—at least not in front of other people—but it had been a whirlwind of a month and I felt a rush of loneliness come over me. I missed my dad.

"Dear? I don't understand?" Dorothy broke the silence.

I sighed. "This is a creepy game you all are playing. Please just stop, okay?" My voice was shaking now.

"What are you talking about?" Minnie stepped toward me this time and placed my hand between hers. Her eyes searched mine.

"Trixie! You all acting like you can't see her and telling me she's dead! This is nuts!" I yanked my hand away, instantly feeling a pang of guilt because I could tell by Minnie's face that I'd hurt her feelings. I tried to grab Trixie's arm. I say tried because I wasn't able to. My hand went right through her and I lost my balance.

I must've missed, I thought. I reached for her again, looking more carefully this time, and watched my hand pass right through her again. The air felt a bit heavier there, but that was it. I decided that I was obviously hallucinating. I'd never hallucinated before, and it was terrifying. *Could dehydration cause hallucinations? What about exhaustion? Exhaustion definitely could. Oh God, was I suffering from heat stroke? But wait, how could I hallucinate a dead girl I'd never met or heard of before? That didn't make any sense either.*

I looked at Trixie closely. She didn't look like a ghost. At least not how they're portrayed in the movies and tv. She wasn't semi-see-through. She didn't have obvious wounds to indicate how she died. She didn't look scary at all.

She just looked like a regular girl. Except she wasn't.

"Dru?" Heather said my name with hesitation. I turned around slowly to a trio of bewildered faces.

Minnie broke the silence. "Can you hear her?" Her eyes widened. "Can you *see* her?"

I closed my eyes tightly and faced Trixie's direction before opening them again. Yes, she was still there.

"Yes," I managed to whisper.

Trixie gave me a sympathetic look. "Don't be scared."

I turned back to see that Minnie was beaming. I looked to Dorothy, the seemingly sane one, and she too had a smile creeping onto her face. Heather was my only hope. I glanced in her direction and our eyes locked. She smiled, but there was a hint of something else there. I wondered if maybe she was just as confused as I was.

"I don't understand," I choked out. And at that moment, the tears came flooding. The ones I'd held in as I tried to be strong over the loss of my fiancé, my best friend, my mother, my grandmother, my identity.

Over the sound of my sobs I heard Dorothy say, "She has her grandmother's gift."

CHAPTER 3

*M*y eyes felt dry as I opened them, and it took me a second to register where I was. I vaguely remembered being brought upstairs and put to bed, almost as if it were a dream or a memory from long ago. Someone had stayed with me and held my hand and I must've fallen asleep. I knew it couldn't have been too long as the pillow was still wet from my tears, but the sun had gone down and the room was dark.

I noticed a framed picture on the bedside table, lit by the moonlight coming in through the windows. In it was a tiny little woman with shocking white hair and a huge smile spread across her face, standing in front of the bookstore. She wore wide-framed glasses, complete with a long beaded neck string. I couldn't help but think that she was absolutely adorable, and I realized that she must be my grandmother. I grinned at the fact that she'd kept a picture of herself next to her bed.

Then I noticed the other picture on the nightstand, a bit farther back. I had never seen any pictures of my mother, but I was certain this was her. She had my snow-white hair, the red tendril peeking out in bits through the weaving of a loose side braid. She stared down smiling, a look of adoration in her eyes, at the small baby in her arms. Me. I felt my eyes begin to well.

"Finally!" a voice interrupted my thoughts. "Glad you're up. I was getting bored." I sat up and squinted around the dark room but didn't see anyone. It wasn't a voice I recognized, but then again, I'd only been here a few hours.

"Hello?" My voice was hoarse.

"Yes, hellooo." The voice sounded annoyed.

"Heather?"

"Try again."

"Trixie?" I whispered. My head felt foggy.

"Do I really sound like a pre-menopausal woman to you?"

It registered now. She was right. Definitely the voice of a much older woman.

"Dorothy? Minnie?"

She made a noise, "No. Tweedledee and Tweedledum left hours ago. Jeez, will you turn on the light, for Pete's sake?"

Honestly, I was afraid to turn on the light. Three days ago, I would've jumped up, demanded to know who was in the room, and promptly kicked them out. After all, they were in *my* (new) home, but seeing a ghost changes your perspective. After the day I'd had, I wasn't sure I could take much more shock and I had a feeling that's exactly what was coming.

"Go on," she chided. "I'm not scary. In fact, it's less disturbing if you just turn on the light." It's like she read my mind. I reached over to the lamp on the bedside table and pulled its golden beaded cord. Light sprang into the room, but I still hesitated to turn around.

I decided to stand first, not knowing who or what was behind me. *Please don't be another ghost, please don't be another ghost,* I pleaded silently. I turned with hesitation until I was looking at a little old woman standing in the middle of the room. She was swimming in a simple floral print dress, an oversized blue cardigan, and thick nude pantyhose.

I instantly recognized her. It was the old woman from the picture on the nightstand.

She held her arms out wide. "See? I'm not scary at all."

"Are you my grandmother?" I managed to say.

"No, I'm the cleaning lady," she scoffed. "Yes, of course I am! Surprise!" she threw her arms out wide and shuffled her feet in a little dance. Her pristine white tennis shoes didn't make a sound against the tiled floor. *Of course I am?* She said that like seeing your recently deceased grandmother was just a regular Monday.

The wide array of emotions I was feeling must've passed over my face, because her voice softened. "I'm really happy to see you again, baby girl. Although I wish it were under better circumstances." She paused. "You're as beautiful as your mother was."

A bird cawed from the corner of the room and I jumped.

"Oh, don't let this loudmouth scare you." She walked over to the birdcage, and I could see a raven perched inside. "She's domesticated." Granny let out a laugh then and the bird cawed in unison.

"But you're dead?" I was still really having a hard time grasping the whole ghost thing.

"Dead as a doornail, I'm afraid. Which makes me as mad as a mule chewing on bumblebees. I had plenty of good years left in me." She scowled. I still had no idea how she'd actually died. I had assumed natural causes of some sort, given her age, and her lawyer had never offered more than 'she passed.'

"Hopefully this isn't a sore subject," I ventured, "but how exactly did you die?"

"How did I die?!" she was incredulous. It was a sore subject.

"What in the world is going on around here? Did no one tell you anything?!"

Okay, I could see the 'spitfire' reference now.

"No, not really, to be honest. My dad, the lawyer, your friends from earlier—it seems I've been kept in the dark about a lot of things."

She shook her head. "All right, honey, let me break down the basics for you—" The raven interrupted her with a loud caw.

"No, stop, this is important. She needs to know," she said to the raven.

"As you know, I'm dead. Although I was definitely murdered. I think. Two, you can see ghosts, but you've already figured that out. I know it's strange. You'll get used to it. Three, you have this ability because of number four." She paused to adjust the glasses on her face, "And number four, you're a witch. I'm—was—a witch. Your mother was a witch. The gals you met downstairs earlier, Trixie included, are witches too."

She threw her hands in the air. "Everyone's a witch!" She smiled. "Not funny? Lighten up. Anyway, you come from a very long line of witches. Not only a long line, but a powerful one. One of the most powerful in the world actually." She said that last part with pride and crossed the room to a small table underneath the window across from me and sat, or rather hovered an inch above the chair next to it.

"Any questions?" she asked.

I didn't even know where to start. "But witches aren't real—"

"Says who?"

"I don't know. Everyone?"

"Then they're wrong." She shrugged. "You don't have to believe me. I mean, you are talking to a ghost, after all," she rolled her eyes, "but you'll see for yourself soon enough."

She turned suddenly to the raven. "Will you quiet down? Now is not the time." Granny barked.

"Wait, is that bird talking to you? Can you talk to animals?"

"Yes, well, all ghosts can, actually. But I could when I was alive too. You'll get there eventually yourself... now that you're here." I must've had a disbelieving look on my face because she proceeded, "What? Seeing ghosts is fine, talking to your dead grandmother is fine, and discovering you're a witch is borderline but tolerable, but you draw the line at talking animals?"

She motioned to Maui, perched on the bed staring in her direction. "By the way, your cat is hungry. He hasn't shut up about it since he got here." She paused. "Also, he's kind of a jerk." Maui and I looked at each other and I couldn't help but burst out laughing.

"This is nuts! All of this is absolutely nuts!" I was overcome with so many emotions, but I was laughing so hysterically I had to sit back down on the bed.

"I know it's a lot to take in," Granny started. There was a serious tone to her voice that brought me back to reality. My new reality. I wiped the tears under my eyes and pulled Maui into my lap, stroking his silky black fur.

She continued, "Most of us, witches that is, we know what we are from birth. We grow up around magic, some of us talking to animals and ghosts and the like. It's normal for us. Your parents had every intention of raising you the same way, but after your mother's death..." her voice caught. Could ghosts cry? "It was best if your father took you far from here. Gave you a chance to have a normal life. I hated it, but I knew it needed to happen. We had to keep you safe, see?" she looked down at her lap. "But I thought about you every single day."

"But you left everything to me. That meant I had to come back?"

"No, I didn't." She shook her head and paused to adjust her glasses. "I never made a will or anything like that. As I said, I had a lot of life left in me. I suppose I probably would've ended up leaving it to you, but I wasn't worrying about that decision until I needed to. That was stupid of me, I guess." That last part looked like it pained her to say.

"I don't understand. When your lawyer called, he specifically referenced a living trust."

"Which further solidifies the idea that something fishy is going on around here," she said, crossing her arms over her chest.

"Yes, it does."

"You know, part of me always wanted you to come back. While I agreed with your father taking you away from here while you grew up, we disagreed strongly on whether or not he should tell you who you are one day. He wanted to get you far away and fast. We never saw eye-to-eye on that. I felt you deserved to know the truth about where you came from and let the choice be yours to make. You know, you're the sole surviving member of our family now."

"Really? No aunts or cousins or anything?" I asked.

"Nope. Just you, kid. No pressure."

"So, how does this work exactly then? Do I have a bunch of powers that I've just been completely unaware of or something?"

"Sort of. I'm sure things have happened that you couldn't quite explain, but you brushed them off at the time?"

"Yeah, because witches and magic and ghosts and talking animals aren't real. So how does this work then? Do I get a wand now or does magic just shoot out of my finger?" I said sarcastically.

"Hilarious," she rolled her eyes.

"I'm just wondering what kind of magical powers I have and how they work."

"Well, I have no idea," she said. "You can see ghosts, we know that. I have an idea of what else might be coming your way, but the rest of your powers will come to you a little bit at a time so as not to overwhelm you all at once. Magic is kind like that." She winked.

"How do I suddenly have this magic power that I never had before though? And why is it going to get even stronger now that I'm here? I don't understand."

"It's complicated, which is why you should grow up learning these lessons," Granny sighed, "but in layman's terms, magic is really just energy. And energy is eternal and infinite. You were born with a special kind of energy because of your birthright. Once one of your ancestors dies, that energy has to go somewhere. You following?"

I nodded.

"So, when I was ripped from this world far too early, my energy was transferred to you. Along with all the energy I possessed from each of my ancestors," she explained.

"But what if someone doesn't have anyone to pass the energy onto?" I interrupted.

"Then the energy goes back into mother earth to distribute as she pleases. She has always been very favorable to our line, by the way, so be kind to her."

I winced remembering the candy wrapper I'd thrown out my car window on the way there.

"This place—Blackwood Bay—is a hotbed of magical energy. One of the most magical places in the world. Even humans can tap into it if they know what they're doing. There's a long story there, but it's not relevant now. Anyway, you'll be far more powerful now that you're here *and* you've got my magic as well."

"So, Trixie, her energy—magic—just went back into the universe, basically?"

Granny nodded.

"What happened to her?" I asked, softly. I couldn't see her but I didn't know if she was present. I wasn't sure how the whole ghost thing worked yet.

"She was twenty-two years old. What do you think happened to her?"

I gave her a quizzical look.

Granny threw up her arms. "She was murdered! Same as me." She jabbed her finger at her chest.

"But how? And why? Why would someone kill either one of you?"

"How am I supposed to know?" She shrugged.

"Gee, I don't know. You just got through telling me about how you were the most powerful witch ever in all the land. Seems you might know *something*." I rolled my eyes.

She groaned. "It doesn't work that way. You watch too much TV. Feed that darn cat, will you? He's driving me nuts."

Oops, I forgot all about feeding Maui.

"Sorry, kitty," I said and went about finding a can of cat food in my luggage.

"Look, when a witch is old and approaching the end of her life, she knows she's not long for this world. Gives her time to get her things in order and say her goodbyes. But when a witch is stolen from this world, she's not given the same luxury." Granny said.

I popped open Maui's can of food and set it next to the bed. "So do witches get murdered a lot?" I asked. Like I really needed to add 'murder' to my list of things to worry about.

She shook her head, "No, the world is generally a good place and others are generally good, but it does happen. We do have evil witches—we call them dark witches—and we have enemies that fear us and assume we're all evil, but on the whole we live a very peaceful existence and try to bring good to the world. Just like regular humans do."

"Okay, so someone definitely murdered Trixie, and we'll assume someone murdered you—"

"No, they did," she said adamantly. "I was as healthy as a horse! I was just sitting there enjoying a piece of cheesecake and the next thing I know, I woke up dead!"

I stilted my laughter. "Okay, so who do you know that might want to kill a sweet little old lady," I glanced at her out of the corner of my eye to see if she caught my sarcasm, but she gave me a blank stare, "and a young woman?"

"Could be anyone. Just because two women who just so happened to be witches were killed in the same town doesn't mean much. They may not even be related. That's what you need to figure out."

"*Me?*"

"Yes, you."

"Isn't that what the police are for?" I asked.

She waved her hand dismissively. "They're all right, but there hasn't been much murdering around here in the last hundred years or so. Besides they don't have what you have."

"And what's that?"

"Haven't you been working the last few years as a private investigator for your dad's firm? Must mean you have, at the very least, some basic investigative skills." *Shoot, how did she know that? Oh right, she's a witch.* "You've also got a whole coven of practiced witches behind you and, best of all," she smiled, "you've got magic."

CHAPTER 4

$\mathcal{I}$ had gotten virtually no sleep the night before. Granny insisted on 'lessons,' which basically just consisted of her trying to teach me how to 'hold' my magical energy, breaking my concentration, and then yelling at me for doing it wrong. Sorry, lady, but I've known I was a witch for like two hours—I'm doing my best.

At some point she finally gave up and told me to get some rest. But between her arguing with Maui and the raven interspersed with mumbling to herself all night, I managed only a few hours of sleep. I gave up around 7 a.m., but since the lawyer's office didn't open until nine, I had plenty of time for a long, hot shower—*finally*—and a few strong cups of coffee. Thankfully, Granny had the good stuff.

The night before, I had told her all about the Fake-Dru and to say she was angry was a huge understatement. She had ordered me to march my butt down to the lawyer's office and tell him he better get this straightened out or else. I wished she was able to do it for me, because for such a tiny little woman, she was scary as hell. "You have to speak up for yourself. No one else in this world is going to do it for you!" she lectured. Maui had passed out by that point but woke up to start arguing with her again sometime around three o'clock.

She had asked me to put her 'stories,' aka soap operas, on for her before I left and she was too engrossed in them to notice I was getting ready to leave.

"All right, I'm off like a wedding dress!" I called out, closing the door. The wooden steps creaked under my feet as I bounded down to the first level of the building. I heard rustling as I opened the door separating the stairwell from the bookstore, and I saw Heather standing near a corner window, unpacking wind chimes. I noticed there was an alarming number of them; the entire storefront was lined with rows of them. *Maybe it's some witch thing,* I thought.

"Good morning!" Heather said brightly. "How'd you sleep?"

I groaned and rolled my eyes.

She chuckled. "Granny keep you up all night I'm guessing?"

"Wait, how'd you know Granny was... here? Is it because you're a—you know, too?" I wasn't sure if there was some rule about whether or not I was allowed to say it.

"I am." She nodded. "A witch that is. Dorothy and Minnie too. And Trixie was." A look of grief washed over her face, but it passed just as quickly, "We actually have quite a few in this town and you'll be meeting them all sooner or later. Just as a heads up, most of the people that will come into this store are too, whether they're local or tourists. Eventually you'll be able to tell, once you get a better handle on your witchy ways." She chuckled at herself. "As for your Granny, she didn't tell you about what happens when there's a transfer of family energy?"

She studied my face for a moment. "Ha. Of course she

didn't." She shook her head, "When a witch passes and she has a successor, she has to stick around until they know everything they need to. It's a lot of new magic to acquire all at once, usually coupled with new powers too, so the old witch has to sort of mentor her protégé, so to speak. Witch ghosts can go back and forth between this world and the next once it's completed. But until then they're bound to it—or to their predecessor—until she learns all she needs to know and masters her newfound magic. It can be pretty disastrous otherwise."

"So, what? She's like Obi-Wan Kenobi?" I joked.

Heather snorted.

"Yeah, she didn't mention that part."

Heather looked at me expectantly, anticipating my next question.

"So how long does that usually take?" Not that I didn't like having her around, and not that I wasn't excited to get to know her, but suddenly having an eighty-year-old roommate and never any privacy... Yikes.

Heather burst out laughing. "Oh, honey." She gave me a sympathetic look and proceeded to laugh even harder.

"That long, huh?"

"Only because you're new to all of this." She gave my arm a quick pat. "We'll all help you though. We'll turn you into a fast learner and you'll have it down in no time. Don't you worry." She gave me an encouraging smile.

"Thanks." I felt a small sense of relief.

"Well, I'm headed to see Granny's lawyer." I waved.

"Good luck!" she exclaimed. "Oh, Dru? Once you get settled in the next few days, do you think we could discuss what you want to do about the store?" she asked.

I didn't understand.

"I mean, don't get me wrong, I love working here but, now

37

that Trixie's gone, I'm the only employee. I just was curious if you wanted to hire someone else or I'd be happy to train you to work here. But as much as I love this place, being the only employee might severely impair my personal life." She smiled.

"Oh, of course! Yes, I'm so sorry, Heather. I hadn't even thought about that. Sorry, I'm still getting used to everything. And I've never been a business owner before."

"Totally understandable. You've been hit with a tidal wave of new information in the last twenty-four hours. I wouldn't expect you to have it all figured out yet."

"Thanks, Heather."

"No problem," she said with a smile and turned back to her wind chimes. I left the store feeling hopeful that I'd made my first real friend in this strange town.

～

*B*lackwood Bay was the epitome of a cute little town. It was right off of the coast and offered all the beauty of the Pacific Northwest. You could walk straight to the beach from the main strip and I was already in love with the soft, salty breeze and beautiful view.

The streets were lined with cobblestones and buildings that were hundreds of years old, all looking as if they'd been carefully restored to maintain their vintage charm. Main Street was adorned with kitschy shops, antique stores, and locally owned restaurants and cafés. It seemed everything was within walking distance, which was something I'd have to get used to coming from a large suburban city, but I had a feeling I'd like it very much. Plus, once I returned the rental car, I'd have no choice.

I came to the crosswalk on the corner and noticed a man standing near the alley behind the bookstore. Blackwood Bay was certainly a tourist town and quite bustling even on a week-day, but the fact that he turned away abruptly when I spotted him gave me an uneasy feeling. A chill ran up my back and my lifetime spent as a private investigator's daughter instinctively made me take note of his appearance: average height and build, black jacket, bushy gray beard, and a navy baseball hat with a shark jumping through a life preserver. It was already approaching eighty degrees at only nine o'clock, so the jacket seemed a bit out of place.

He might've been a tourist, but something about him still gave me pause. I hurried across the street and headed away from the Port itself, following the directions on my phone's GPS. I glanced back but the man was gone. Having seen two ghosts over the last twenty-four hours was certainly messing with my creepy sensors. I rounded the corner to head up Foxglove Street, which contained a row of office buildings, when I ran smack dab into a wall that I was certain hadn't been there a second ago. I bounced back and was startled to see Wolf Harper standing in front of me, a big toothy grin on his face.

"Well, good morning to you too," he teased.

"Ah, sorry. I was distracted trying to follow these directions on my phone." I waved my phone, feeling a rush of heat in my cheeks.

"No worries." He smiled and put his hand on his hips. He looked good in his uniform. Like, really good. "I don't have your tire back yet, but I was actually planning on stopping in today to see how you were settling in."

"You check in on all the new transplants around here, Deputy? Sergeant?" I teased but I wasn't sure of his official title.

"Ha, no. It's Sergeant, by the way. I'm actually a recent transplant myself. I've only been here a few weeks, so I'm no master, but the chief has lived here his whole life and he's done a fine job filling me in on all the best local spots to eat." He patted his stomach. He did have a small pooch, I noticed. Cute though.

"Oh, I thought you said you knew my grandmother?" I asked.

He scrunched up his brow. "Sorry?"

"When we first met yesterday. You said you knew my grandmother."

"Did I?" He clenched his jaw.

"You did. Did you move here right before she died or something?" I asked.

He nodded, relaxing his forehead. "Yeah, I didn't get a chance to know her long. My loss, I'm sure." He smiled.

"Well, I'd love to hear your restaurant recommendations sometime." I fidgeted with the ring on my finger. Why did this man make me so nervous?

"Great. It's a date!" He quickly added, "Well, I'd better get going. Apparently, Mrs. Powders' chickens got loose and they're hopping around and pooping all over the place over at Mr. Chase's. Seems she's not home at the moment either. He's pretty pissed."

I laughed. "Wow. Some serious police work going on in this town."

"It's a nice change, that's for sure. See you." *Change from what*, I wondered? He patted my shoulder as he walked past and I felt a surge in my stomach. Those were really starting to get annoying.

Wait, did I just agree to a date? Or was it like one of those things where you just say 'it's a date' but it's not *really* a real date? Crap. I had no idea. But I could figure that out later, it was already after nine o'clock and the lawyer's office was open.

I hurried up the street until I saw a wooden sign posted in a small patch of grass that read: POWDERS AND BURNS, ATTORNEYS AT LAW. I wondered if the chickens belonged to Powders' mother. I mean, how many Powders could there possibly be in this town?

I walked up the uneven brick steps and pushed open the sticky door to his office. The bell slammed angrily against it, announcing my arrival. See, businesses have bells on their doors! A young woman sat behind the front desk and glanced over at me with annoyance, as I had inadvertently interrupted her taking a picture of herself with her cell phone. She was heavily made-up and posing with a fake pout in attempt to make her lips appear larger than they really were.

"Can I help you?" She sounded as if the last thing she wanted to do was help me.

"I'm here to see Mitch Powders."

"Oh, he's not in." She went back to her phone.

"Okay, well when will he be back?"

"Not really sure."

It felt like I was pulling teeth.

"Fine. Then I'll just wait," I said.

"Gonna be waiting a while," she smirked.

I closed the gap between us and sat my heavy purse down on the space in front of her. I was trying to take a cue from Granny's playbook.

"Listen. I've already spoken with him on the phone once before. My grandmother was a client of his and I've inherited her estate, but I still need to sign paperwork and I have a serious matter to discuss with Mr. Powders. It's urgent and I'm not interested in playing twenty questions with you. Can you give me *any* information at all or are you going to keep up the Cheshire Cat routine?" I said with as much snark as possible.

She rolled her eyes. "All I know is I came into work two days ago and he'd left a note on my desk that said he was going on vacation and wasn't sure when he'd be back. It said to cancel his appointments for the next week. He said he'd call, but I haven't heard from him yet and he's not answering *my* calls so..." she trailed off.

"Okay, well what about his partner? Burns? Can he help me?" I asked.

"Probably not, since they don't share clients. But Mr. Burns isn't here either. He's on a cruise with his family and won't be back for at least a week."

"Great." I sighed.

"Here." She handed me a business card with Mitch Powders' cell number on it. "Maybe you'll have better luck than me." And with that, she went back to her phone, obviously dismissing me.

I muttered a thanks on my way out the door. How in the world was I supposed to clear this whole Fake-Dru thing up now? A girl shows up claiming to be me and there's a living trust that my grandmother never even had made. The two obviously had to be connected somehow and I'd have to find the rest of the puzzle pieces myself, it seemed. Moving to this town was proving to be more stressful than I could've ever anticipated.

I contemplated calling my father then. If anyone could help me with this mess it was him, but I just wasn't ready for all of the emotions that phone call would dredge up, so I promised myself I'd do it later that afternoon. My stomach growled and I decided to stop in at a sweet-looking little place I'd passed on my way to Mitch Powders' office.

*P*eaches' Café sat just a few storefronts up from the bookstore. The outside of the building had been painted a, well, peach color so it was hard to miss. I'd tried calling Mitch Powders' cell phone number three times on my walk over, but it went to voicemail every single time.

Frustrated, I threw my cell back into my purse and walked inside the café. The place was shockingly busy and I worried that I might actually have to wait for a table. I contemplated leaving but just as I was about to turn and head for the door, someone approached.

"Is it just you?" a girl with long lavender-colored hair asked. She couldn't have been any older than twenty, though it was hard to accurately guess with the heavy dark makeup around her eyes. She had one of those bull ring nose piercings and small silver studs on either side of her face where her dimples were supposed to be.

"Uh, yeah. Just me."

"You can sit up at the counter then." She smiled and grabbed a menu and I noticed her arm was covered in intricate tattoos featuring both skulls and vibrantly colored flowers. I hurried behind her.

She brought me to the back of the café, directly in front of the kitchen. The first half of the counter we passed was a huge glass case filled with some of the most delicious looking desserts I'd ever seen: cheesecakes, pies, eclairs, cookies, cupcakes, fudge. In the middle was a waist-high swinging door and cash register, and next to it a white marble countertop in front of swiveling diner-esque bar stools. She set my menu down in front of the peach-colored stool nearest the pastry case and I decided at that moment that I was definitely taking some treats home with me. As I drooled over the desserts, I missed the woman coming to stand in front of me.

"Morning, darlin'! Coffee?" I heard a welcoming Southern drawl and turned my attention to the woman behind the counter. If there was an actual Peaches who owned this place, this *had* to be her. I guessed she was probably in her fifties, though it was hard to tell exactly with the contoured makeup and vibrant purple and blue shades of eyeshadow she was wearing. She was full-figured in a deep V-cut lavender sweater, cinched around her waist with a sparkling silver belt. Her blueish-gray hair was styled just to the middle of her neck and looked like it had been on the losing end of a fight with a large can of hairspray. Not a single hair seemed out of place.

"Yes, that'd be great," I said.

She leaned in close and rested her elbows on the counter in front of me, the silver hoops in her ears swinging. "So happy to have you here, sweetie. I knew your mama, and of course your grandmama, my whole life. Always wondered how Aurora's daughter turned out. You're just as lovely as she was." Peaches' eyes got a little misty.

"How did you know I was Aurora's daughter?" It felt strange meeting people who knew my mother when I never did. Peaches winked at me, her brilliant blue eyes containing a hint of mischief, and she turned to grab the coffeepot on the counter behind her.

I had to wonder if she was trying to convey something she couldn't say out loud, like that maybe she was a witch too, but I was hesitant to make any rash assumptions. It easily could've been my distinctive hair that gave me away. It also didn't seem likely that nearly every woman I'd met in this town so far was a witch. There really needed to be some sort of secret way to ask someone this question.

Peaches placed a mug in front of me and began to pour my coffee, "Well, if you haven't figured it out yet, I'm Peaches. My real name is Georgia, by the way, but no one really calls me that. And I see you've met my oldest daughter, Electra," the stack of silver bangle bracelets on her wrist jingled as she motioned to the lavender-haired girl, "and that over there is my baby, Astra." She turned and pointed to a girl near the end of the counter.

Astra had the same long hair as her sister, but hers was a pastel pink. She didn't have any piercings or tattoos like her sister, but their features were otherwise identical. Astra gave me a smile and a little wave before she went back to taking someone's order.

Peaches set the sugar and a small carafe of cream in front of me. "I was sure hopin' you'd pop in soon. I heard you just got into town yesterday." Anticipating my next question, she said, "Dorothy and Minnie told me—anyway, I was hopin' to get to meet you before the meeting this week. There'll be a whole gaggle of hens there and I wanted to have you all to myself for a few minutes. I'm selfish that way." She smiled, and her teeth were so white that I knew she'd either recently had them professionally whitened or she paid a pretty penny for some veneers.

"Gaggle of hens?" I stirred the sugar and cream around in my mug.

She laughed. "It's what my late husband—rest his sweet soul—used to call it when a bunch of women got together. A Hen Party, he'd say, loud and everyone bawking all at once." We both chuckled.

"I like that metaphor. I think I'll use it myself." I sipped my coffee. "So, I don't think I've been informed of this, although it might've slipped my mind as it's been a very overwhelming eighteen hours, but what meeting exactly?"

Peaches' eyes widened. "Oh, goodness. Well, we all get together every Wednesday for what we call book club."

"Who is *we*?"

"Just the local hens who all have something very... special, in common." Her eyes darted around the cafe. "We meet at Granny's—uh, *your*—bookstore. Hence it being a 'book club' meeting." She winked.

Okay, at this point I was thinking it was safe to assume that she was a witch.

"I think I understand." I nodded slowly.

"Could you be any more obvious, Mama?" Electra came up beside her mother and rolled her eyes, her hair color almost a perfect match for her mother's lavender sweater.

"Oh, hush. Electra here will be there too." She jabbed her thumb in her daughter's direction, "So will her sister."

"Is it a large group then?" I asked. I wasn't sure I was up for hosting a Hen Party quite yet.

"Hmm... well, not everyone comes every week, even though they're *supposed to*. Your Granny wasn't one that anyone wanted to disappoint." Peaches laughed. "Anywho, Dorothy and Minnie—they're sisters, in case you didn't know —recently they've had a habit of comin' irregularly, but that's usually due to Minnie's foibles and Dorothy having to clean up after her. She's a terrible cook."

Electra mouthed 'cook' and made air quotes. I guessed it must be code for doing magic. I mentally patted myself on the back because I was starting to learn some lingo.

Peaches continued, "But now that Granny's gone—oh, I am so sorry about that, sweetie. So sorry for your loss," she put her hand over mine, "but now that Granny's gone, I have a feeling those two will make a better practice out of showing up. Heck, they'll be there with bells on." She rolled her eyes. "You didn't hear this from me," Peaches leaned in close, "but Dorothy always did want to be the Queen Bee." She raised her eyebrows at me like she'd just offered me the winning lottery number.

"What does that mean exactly?" I asked.

"Well, you know, your Granny ran this town and the members of the.... book club. Her and Dorothy grew up together and while they fought like sisters most of the time, I always had a sneaking suspicion that Dorothy was jealous of your grandmama." After my meeting with Dorothy yesterday, I had to admit that surprised me. I made a mental note to ask Granny about it later.

"Stop gossiping, mother." Astra had approached now, rolling her eyes the exact same way as her sister.

"It's not gossip. I don't gossip!" Peaches looked offended.

"Ignore her," Astra butted in. "She *loves* to gossip."

"Lives for it, really," Electra interjected.

"If you two don't hush, I'll have to tongue tie you both again." Electra and Astra looked at each other wide-eyed.

"I don't gossip." She turned back to me. "I just know things. I mean, yes, people tell me almost everything about their lives and I keep those secrets to myself, of course. I'm just *very* observant too." She nodded in agreement with herself. I had a feeling she didn't keep those secrets to herself though, which might prove to be beneficial to me.

"What do you know about Mitch Powders? The lawyer," I asked suddenly.

"Oh! Well, what do you want to know?" she leaned her elbows on the counter again. "You askin' about his divorce? Not his fault, really, I don't think. If you ever met his wife, you'd know she's an easy bake oven, that one." I laughed at the reference I wasn't entirely sure I understood.

"No, no. Although, I'm sure it's all very interesting. I just wondered how he is as a businessman? Is he ethical?" I definitely had my suspicions that the Fake-Dru and Mitch Powders were in on some elaborate scheme. Maybe she'd offered him money in exchange for… something. Fake documents? I didn't know yet.

She looked thoughtful for a moment. "Yes, he is. Mitch is a good man. And if he wasn't, his mama would tan his hide. Doesn't matter how old he is. That woman don't take no crap from nobody."

"Have you heard anything about him going on vacation for an indefinite amount of time?"

"All I heard was when his receptionist came in yesterday. She was whining about how he hadn't given her advance notice. But I don't know much other than that. Wish I did." She shrugged and I believed her. Seemed I'd hit another dead end. I noticed the café's noise was dwindling down and looked around to see that the morning breakfast rush was over.

"Can I ask you something else?" I lowered my voice.

"Oh, anything, sugar." Peaches' eyes lit up.

"What do you know about Granny's death? Have you heard anything? Mitch didn't say how she died and I kind of assumed it was just due to her age, but…" I trailed off.

Peaches glanced around the café to make sure no one was in earshot. "Did you ask her yourself?"

"Yeah, but she doesn't know anything other than being adamant that it was… not a natural death, if you catch my drift. I was hoping maybe you'd heard something?"

She nodded vigorously. "See, I just so happen to have a bit of a… harmless flirtation with the police chief," she started.

"They pretty much fall all over themselves around each other." Electra was at her mother's side again.

Peaches bumped her daughter with her hip. "Anyway, give

that man one of my homemade peach pies and he's pretty much at my mercy."

"I hope that's literal and not a euphemism for something else." Electra stuck her finger in her mouth in a fake gagging motion, but Peaches ignored her.

"See, at first they thought your Granny just had a heart attack. She was eighty-four, after all, but us gals," she motioned to herself and then to me, "we can have a longer than above average lifespan that regular folk don't know about. Your Granny was also as healthy as could be, so some of us just knew that she didn't die the way they were saying, so we pressed the police for an autopsy." She turned away and grabbed a plate of food from the hot counter behind her and set it in front of me. "Still waitin' for the results though they should be in soon, I'd think."

I looked at the plate in front of me: scrambled eggs with ham, cheese, and spinach, salsa on top, and buttered wheat toast with grape jelly. This was the exact breakfast I liked to make for myself at home and she hadn't even taken my order. I looked up at Peaches and she gave me a wink and a knowing smile.

I sipped my coffee as I formulated my next question. "Can I ask what you know about the girl they found yesterday. Trixie?" I was hoping she would pay me another visit herself, but just in case she didn't, I needed to find out what I could.

Peaches frowned and lowered her eyes. "Such a sweet little thing. Good friend to both of my girls."

I looked to Electra who already had tears forming in her eyes. "We *will* find out who hurt her. That I do know." Her voice was shaky and barely above a whisper.

"I'm so sorry. I didn't mean to upset either one of you." I realized I was probably being insensitive. I'd spent my entire adult life working for my dad as a private investigator and I had a tendency to forego social conventions in favor of garnering information.

"We know you didn't." Peaches put her arm around Electra's waist and pulled her close. "We all loved Trixie. If that girl ever had a thought it'd die of loneliness, but she was the salt of the earth."

"Do you know what happened to her?" I ventured.

"I know they found her in the alleyway behind her house. Out by the garbage cans. Poor thing. And it wasn't an accident. That I do know."

"Who found her?" I interjected.

"Local garbage crew. No one really even knew she was missing yet. They just happened to stumble on her while making their weekly rounds."

I thought about how Dorothy had known there was a body to be found in the first place, if no one even knew Trixie was missing yet.

"You said no one really even knew she was missing yet—did you all have your suspicions though? I'm just curious because of something Dorothy said."

Peaches raised her eyebrows and spoke barely above a whisper, "Mmhmm… Dorothy has a feel for those types of things. She stopped in the day before yesterday to let us know. Guess she'd been by Trixie's to check on her but no one answered the door."

I decided not to tell Peaches I'd seen Trixie myself. If I was going to get to the bottom of all of this, I needed to gather information, not share it. Only three people, well, living people, knew I had seen her and I wanted to keep it that way for a while.

"Gosh, that's really just terrible. Do you think the two—my

Granny's death and Trixie's—might be related somehow?" I looked back up to Peaches, but her gaze was fixated on whoever had just walked through the door. I turned to see a woman roughly Peaches' age, but she emitted less of a sweet, sassy vibe and more of a killer businesswoman one. She had her black hair in a sleek pixie cut and her face was framed with large black sunglasses.

"Cheris Sterling," Peaches whispered, "local hotel mogul. And I don't mean the big chain ones you saw on your drive in either. She owns every inn, hotel, and bed and breakfast in this town."

Cheris made her way toward the dessert case, her black designer purse resting on her forearm. She seemed to glide as she walked, her black heels clicking along the floor. She smiled as she approached and the smell of expensive perfume permeated my nose. "Good morning, Peaches." I noticed her black blazer and pencil skirt looked tailored.

Peaches nodded. "What can I get you, Cheris?" Her voice lacked the same tone she'd used with me and I wondered if there was some iciness between the two of them.

"Hmm… I'll take a dozen of your eclairs and two of your coffee cakes. If you could slice that up for me that would be fabulous. Management meeting this morning," she explained, waving her hand in the air. Peaches went to work and Cheris turned her attention to me.

"Hello." It was hard to tell with her sunglasses, but I was pretty sure she was looking me up and down and judging. I had semi-dressed up for my meeting with the lawyer, but I instantly felt inferior in my blue shirtdress and nude sandals. I smoothed one hand over my hair in an attempt to tame any inevitable flyaways.

"Good morning." I sounded much more chipper than I actually was. She kept looking at me like she was waiting for something.

"Are you just visiting our little town here?" she finally asked.

"Oh, no, actually. I just moved here. Yesterday, in fact. My grandmother was Drusilla Rathmore... did you know her?"

Cheris frowned but recovered quickly. "So *you're* the other one!" She smiled and gave me a friendly squeeze on the arm. "A young woman came into one of my hotels yesterday just hysterical, claiming that she was Drusilla's granddaughter and there was another girl here pretending to be her. She just went on and on about how no one believed her. I had to give her one of my Xanax, poor thing." She gave a short laugh.

"Well, I'm not sure who that woman is, but this," Peaches interrupted, pointing at me with her silver tongs, "is Drusilla's granddaughter."

Cheris gave her a tight smile and turned back to me. "Hmm... well, I certainly do hope you girls get this figured out. It must be quite trying having someone claim to be you. I'm sure it's all just a misunderstanding." She waved her hand in the air.

I opened my mouth to speak but she turned away and cut me off. "Peaches, please put this on my account." She watched Peaches box up the rest of her order as if I was no longer there. After Peaches handed her the boxes, she turned to me once more. "It was nice meeting you. Good luck with everything." She nodded to me and then to Peaches before she was on her way out.

"She's a real treat, that one. Like a squeaky shopping cart." Peaches rolled her eyes.

"Mmm, yeah, I can tell," I agreed, but I was already

thinking about what she'd just said about the Fake-Dru making a scene.

I was lucky that I had some of Granny's friends on my side, but what did she have? The lawyer was MIA. I knew that much. But she wouldn't be here making a claim if she didn't have something to back up her statements, would she? And had she really gone to the police like she threatened? And if so, that had to mean she had some kind of proof—or false proof. Would I be able to prove that it was false? My head started swimming and I'd lost my appetite. I apologized to Peaches and told her I wasn't feeling well as I dug through my purse for my wallet.

She promptly declined my attempt at paying for my breakfast. "You're family. Family doesn't pay for meals in here," she said and offered to have one of her daughters drive me home. I thought the fresh air might do me good and it was only a few blocks so I thanked her and left.

My mind was racing as I went over all the information Peaches had just supplied me with. I couldn't know for sure yet if she was a reliable source, but she was as good as any I had at the moment. I decided I'd go back to Granny's and let her know about Mitch Powders. Maybe she could think up another idea while I kept trying to reach him. Or maybe she had some special witch ghost powers that could find out where the heck he was hiding. Afterward, I'd stop by the police station and have a chat with them myself. I hate to admit it, but I felt a little wave of giddiness at the possibility of seeing Harper again.

CHAPTER 5

The sign hanging on the door was turned to OPEN, but I didn't see Heather when I entered. I did a quick scan around the room looking for Trixie, but I didn't see her either.

"Hello?" I called out and Heather emerged from behind a bookshelf.

"How'd it go?" she asked.

"Terrible. Apparently, he's away on vacation for who knows how long." I dropped my bag on the glass countertop and sighed.

"Well, that's weird," Heather stated the obvious.

I nodded. "Yeah, something shady is definitely going on around here."

"Maybe you should go upstairs and lie down for a while? I know you didn't get much sleep last night and it might be easier to tackle your next move with a clear, well-rested head." Heather had a point.

"You're right. Thanks. Let me know if you need me, although I doubt I'd be much help around here just yet." I scooped up my bag and headed upstairs. I was hopeful that Trixie might be hiding up there with Granny. I really needed to talk with both of them.

Granny was still fixated on her 'stories' and it didn't appear that she'd moved at all in the time I'd been gone. I didn't see Trixie anywhere.

Granny turned her attention to me. "Well?"

I flopped down on the sofa. "He's out of town and his receptionist doesn't know where he is."

"That snake!" Granny exclaimed. "What's he up to?" She stood now and started pacing.

"I don't know," I offered weakly. My head still felt a little muddled.

"You think he's in cahoots with that little impostor of yours?"

"I think it's certainly a strong possibility, except that there's something that just doesn't make any sense about that. He called me and told me I'd inherited this place as per a living trust you set up. We know that was fake, but why would he contact me if he was in cahoots, as you say, with this other person to give her this building?"

"Good point." Granny looked like she was thinking. "There's got to be something else then that we're just not seeing yet."

"Obviously." I rolled my eyes.

"Well, you need to think harder. Get out there and hit the streets!"

I laughed. "Granny, this isn't an eighties TV cop show."

"Well, it's a good thing. You're certainly no Magnum, PI."

"You know, I thought grandmothers were supposed to be sweet old ladies who loved to bake goodies and knit you an endless supply of sweaters."

"I'm a ghost, dummy!" Granny threw up her arms. "You'll have to make your own crap."

"At least you have the sweet part down," I said sarcastically.

"No one has ever accused me of being anything but." She lifted her chin and I fought the urge to tell her I highly doubted that.

"Look, I really need some rest so I can think clearly. You three kept me up all night." I motioned around the room to the offending parties. Both Maui and the raven refused to make eye contact with me.

"I see you didn't get your father's work ethic then," Granny chided.

I groaned. "Granny, honestly, I have been here less than twenty-four hours. In that time, I've found out I'm a witch that sees ghosts, met my dead grandmother—who can talk to a cat and a bird, by the way—learned that same grandmother very likely was murdered along with another witch, *and* there's a woman running around town claiming to be me. Can I just have, like, an hour without anything life-altering happening?" I pleaded.

The truth was, as much as I wanted to know what happened to Granny and Trixie and who the mystery impostor was, that I didn't want to investigate any of it myself. Going to work for my dad after college had been an easy transition and he'd given me a lot more responsibility as time passed, even letting me handle my own cases the last few years, but I had made the conscious decision to come to Blackwood Bay and leave my old life behind. I wanted to take a long, maybe even permanent break from the chaos of it all, and spend my days running a quiet little bookstore in a cute little town.

As if on cue, I heard loud voices coming from down in the

bookstore, followed by Heather yelling my name up the staircase.

"What now?!" I threw the pillow I'd been cuddling down on the sofa and headed for the door.

I jogged down the creaking wooden steps and heard a flurry of voices all speaking at once. One was particularly shrill and another was a male's voice that sounded a bit familiar. I opened the door leading into the bookstore and saw Heather looking exasperated. The Fake-Dru was standing in front of her, hands on her hips, and Harper was at her side. I couldn't help but think that they actually looked really good together, a regular Ken and Barbie, and I felt a pang of jealousy run through me.

"What's up?" I said, obvious hesitation in my voice.

Harper started to open his mouth, but Fake-Dru beat him to it.

"There she is!" She pointed at me, narrowing her eyes.

Harper cleared his throat and addressed me. "Hi there. Um, it seems we have a bit of a... weird situation here, as I'm sure you know." He offered a kind smile. "This young woman here also claims to be Drusilla Rathmore Davis."

"Yeah, but she's not. Not the right one, anyway." I was getting really tired of saying that.

He nodded. "I'm not really sure what's going on here. Though I fully intend to find out—"

"Oh, I'll tell you what's going on—" Fake Dru interrupted but Harper put up his hand.

"Anyway, she does have a driver's license with the name Drusilla Davis on it, as well as bank cards. Can I assume you do as well?" he asked.

I nodded, completely stunned. This woman really was one hundred percent committed to this.

"Why don't you check?" Fake-Dru challenged him, but he raised his hand again and rolled his eyes.

Just at that moment, the front door swung open, and in strolled another police officer, though he had about thirty years on Harper.

"Harper. Heather." His voice was gruff, like something you'd expect out of an old western movie. He nodded at the two people in the room he knew and then looked back and forth between Fake-Dru and myself, waiting for an introduction.

She shoved her hand in front of him and plastered a huge smile on her face. "Drusilla Rathmore Davis."

"Ah," he gave her hand a quick shake, "one of a few, so I hear." Her face betrayed her as she gave him a scowl, but she recovered, replacing it with a tight smile.

"You the other?" he turned to me.

"I am," I said.

"You sure look an awful lot like Aurora." He turned back to the other Dru and studied each of us for a moment.

"I just look like my father's side of the family is all." Fake-Dru offered. No, in fact, she looked nothing like my father's side of the family at all. The police officer made a grunting noise.

"Anyhow, I'm Chief Carver." He adjusted the waistband of his pants and let his hands rest on his duty belt. "I'm not here about any of that anyway." He hesitated. "Reason I'm here is we got the report back from the medical examiner regarding Granny, uh, the late Drusilla's, death. Since we don't know for certain yet which one of you is really her granddaughter, I suppose I'll just tell the both of you."

He paused like he was unsure if he was allowed to do that or not. I supposed policework in a town like this didn't afford him many opportunities to investigate homicides, so his grasp on proper protocol was undoubtedly rusty. "The ME said that Drusilla died from poisoning."

Fake-Dru gasped.

"Cyanide, to be exact," he continued, side-eyeing her.

"Oh my god," I said. Granny was right. She had been murdered.

"Oh, my poor grandmother!" Fake-Dru wailed, no doubt trying to one-up me.

The chief shot her an agitated look before he continued, "Given this new information and the fact that the two of you both showed up to claim this place in response to her death, we'll be doing a thorough investigation of *all* likely potential suspects."

"You can't possibly think I killed my own poor grandmother! I just got into town yesterday!" Fake-Dru started.

"You both did," Harper interjected.

"We know that you both claim to have gotten here yesterday. As I said, we'll be doing a thorough investigation, not limited to just the two of you, but anyone who knew Granny and had the opportunity to do something like this. That's a long list, unfortunately. Although, I will say that you both will be questioned and your alibis checked," Chief Carver said.

A wave of panic crossed Fake-Dru's face, but she replaced it almost immediately with a sorrowful look. "Well, I for one am glad. I hope you catch whoever did this to my poor old Granny."

"If the ME was able to detect cyanide, wouldn't her time of death narrow down your list of suspects?" I asked.

My father and I had worked a case once where a woman poisoned her philandering husband with cyanide. She'd read online that it was a quick metabolizing poison so that within a few hours of ingestion, it would no longer be detected and everyone would assume he'd suffered a heart attack. What she failed to learn, however, was that all of it is only metabolized *unless* death occurs first. She'd gone way overboard with the dosage and he died almost instantly, leaving behind enough to trace his cause of death back to cyanide and, ultimately, back to her.

Chief Carver eyed me for a moment and I felt the urge to explain myself. "Before I moved here, I worked for my dad as a private investigator. Mostly the typical cheating spouse and money laundering type stuff, but we did get to help with an occasional murder," I offered. As soon as it came out of my mouth, I realized I might not be making the best case for my innocence.

Fortunately, Chief Carver smiled. "How is your dad? We used to run around together quite a bit before... before he left." His voice trailed off.

"He's good. Just busy trying to help catch bad guys." I smiled.

Fake-Dru started to speak, no doubt to let Chief Carver know that it was actually her dad, when Harper said, "To answer your question, yes, her estimated time of death certainly helps, but poison is a bit tricky. We have to consider the possibility that a food or drink item contained the cyanide and it may have been contaminated long before she ever actually consumed it."

I nodded. "That makes sense."

"Who would do something like that? Poison an old woman? Granny didn't even have any enemies," Heather spoke up, a horrified look on her face.

"That we know of," Harper said.

"Do you think Granny's death and Trixie's are related?" I asked.

Chief Carver made a clicking noise with his mouth. "It's a possibility, of course. Although I'm not sure how they would be at this point. The two of them didn't have much in common other than the fact that they both worked at this bookstore." *And that they're witches*, I thought.

I caught Heather looking at me and knew she must've been thinking the same thing.

"So Trixie didn't die the same way?" she asked.

The chief shook his head. "I'm sorry, but I really shouldn't be discussing this with any of you. It's an open murder investigation after all." He lowered his eyes. "Such a terrible thing to happen to such a sweet girl though."

"Wait, someone else was murdered here recently?" Fake-Dru asked.

We all nodded.

"Oh my god, what is this place? Murdertown?"

I laughed and she shot me a look. I guess I misread that comment. She was being serious.

"We never have stuff like this happen around here," the chief said, "until very recently that is." He looked around at each of us again and I guessed that he was trying to get a read on all of us.

"Heather, would you mind coming down to the station tomorrow? I know you and Trixie were rather close and we'd like to ask you a few questions."

Heather nodded. "Yes, of course. I'll be there first thing."

"Well, I'll be in touch," he said to the room and tipped his hat before he walked out the door.

"Wow," Heather said. "I can't believe someone murdered Granny."

"We'll get to the bottom of it," Harper assured her.

"Back to the more pressing issue," Fake-Dru said.

"Sorry?" Harper asked.

"What are we going to do about this impostor trying to steal my inheritance out from under me?" she crossed her arms over her chest and jutted her hip out.

"You're ridiculous." Heather laughed and received a well-practiced scowl in return.

"Ah, right. Well, we could easily clear this up if we could reach your father or if I was able to run a quick search on your driver's licenses, but we seem to be having some serious issues. Tech guys are working hard on it, but it's a bit of a mess—"

Fake-Dru cut him off. "Wait, but you can see my ID is real. It's state-issued."

"Yeah, I can see that it appears to be. But a quick run through the system can give me verifiable proof."

"How so?" she asked. She looked calm but I knew she had to have been sweating bullets.

Harper sighed. "When we run a DL through the system, we can see all of the previous DLs under that name. If one of you is lying, it will be easy to tell since the previous ID pictures will only match one of you."

"But—but what if she paid off the DMV somehow? To, like, mess with the system and have them put in false information?" Fake-Dru asked.

Wow, she was really grasping at straws here.

"That is so highly unlikely that it's not even worth exploring." Harper sighed. "Anyway, we haven't been able to get ahold of Byron Davis and it seems Mr. Powders, Granny's lawyer, is unreachable at the moment as well, so that puts us in a bit of a pickle for tonight. We're also using most of our manpower on two ongoing murder investigations, so this is getting put on the backburner for tonight. However, we will be investigating this situation the first chance we get and I hope to have it sorted out as soon as tomorrow. Whichever one of you is lying is going to be in serious trouble." He took a moment to make eye contact with each of us. "Until then, I suggest neither of you leave town."

"I planned on staying at my grandmother's store—which I *inherited*—so is the police station going to pay my hotel bills? Because that's going to get very expensive," Fake-Dru said. She seemed to have regained her confidence rather quickly.

"Not likely, no," Harper replied.

"That's unfair! She gets to stay here because she happened to get into town and claim it just before I did!"

"All right, all right." Harper put up his hands and shook his head. "Look. I do agree that it's not exactly fair that one of you gets free room and board while we get this straightened out." He paused and I could tell he was hesitant to say what was coming next. "Why don't you both just stay here tonight until we get this whole mess sorted out?"

"Fine by me." Fake-Dru crossed her arms over her chest and smiled smugly.

"What? No way!" Heather chimed in. "We don't even know what she's really after here. I don't want her snooping around and I know Granny wouldn't want her to either."

"I honestly don't know what the alternative solution would be other than having them both go to separate hotels," Harper said.

"No thanks. I'll stay here." Fake-Dru seemed to be challenging me and I wasn't one to back down.

"Me too," I said evenly.

"Great. It's settled then." He sighed and Heather made a disagreeable noise. Just what I needed: another annoying roommate. And Granny? She was *not* going to be happy about this.

CHAPTER 6

"Oh, this broad better get out of here right now!" Granny was already hollering before Fake-Dru and I had even made it through the doorway of the apartment.

"I'm as happy about this as you are," I muttered.

Fake-Dru stood just inside the doorway and assessed the space. Granny's apartment had been set up with convenience in mind. The main level consisted of one giant room, similar to a studio apartment. There was a decent-sized kitchen and eating area, a large living space with a couch, TV, and chairs. Off to one side of the room was an alcove she used as her bedroom. The upper level housed a guest room and additional bathroom, and the rest Granny had left as one large storage space. It was something I would've loved to explore, hoping to find old picture albums and such, but it felt wrong going through Granny's things without asking while she was still here.

"Where's my room?" Fake-Dru asked, as if she were checking in to a bed and breakfast. Maui hissed at her and the raven let out a troubled caw.

"There's a bedroom upstairs you can have." I sat down on the couch.

"No way. Get her out of here! This is... this is treason!" Granny shouted.

I smirked. "It's not treason. It's not even close."

"What are you blabbering on about?" Fake-Dru was half-carrying, half-dragging a suitcase almost as big as she was.

"Nothing." This was going to be a particularly tricky situation. How was I going to talk to Granny with Fake-Dru around? I really needed to tell her what Chief Carver had said about her being poisoned, but I was already being pegged as a potential identity thief. If Fake-Dru reported that I was also talking to imaginary people, I'd be carted off to the nearest mental hospital.

"I'm going upstairs to get settled," she called over her shoulder, as she clomped up the stairs in her tall wedge sandals.

I laid my head down on the arm of the couch and closed my eyes waiting for Granny to start in again, but it never came. I must've dozed off, because I was jolted awake by loud shrieks coming from upstairs. Maui pounced from the back of the couch onto my side, before taking off up the stairs. I stumbled to my feet with the intent to follow, but he was on his way back down a second later. Fake-Dru close behind him, still shrieking.

"What's going on?" I still felt a little out of it from being woken so abruptly. Fake-Dru ran past me before she turned around to answer, her eyes wide. "There's someone up there," she whispered.

"Okay, well, you just ran down the stairs screaming your head off so I'm not sure whispering now will do much good." I ran my hand through my hair and went to grab my taser out of my purse.

"What are you doing?" she said, a horrified look on her face.

"I'm going to check it out," I answered.

"What, no! What if it's, like, a serial killer or something?" she grabbed my arm. She might be trying to steal my identity, but at least she didn't want me dead. Unless... what if she was trying to scare me into leaving?

"What makes you think someone is up there?" I eyed her cautiously, looking for any signs that she might be lying.

"Okay," she stepped closer and lowered her voice, "I was upstairs and I got bored, right? Like, there's no TV up there or anything. So I decided to check out what kind of stuff was in that big room upstairs—the one with all the boxes and stuff—and I heard, like, some rustling noises—"

"It might've just been my cat," I interrupted her and motioned to Maui.

"No, it wasn't. He was sitting in the doorway watching me. It definitely wasn't him. So, anyway, I hear the rustling and I think okay, maybe there's like a mouse up here or something and I *hate* mice, so I decided to get out of there and right then one of those creepy mannequin things—you know, the ones seamstresses use—it came rolling toward me all by itself!"

Granny burst out laughing and I realized she hadn't been in the room with us up until then. "Tell her that's what she gets for snooping through my stuff!"

So it had been Granny messing with her. I can't say I was surprised, but I wasn't sure how to respond to Fake-Dru given this new information.

"Um, are you sure? Maybe there's a logical explanation," I said, not that there was a logical explanation for anything around here.

"I'm sure!" She looked really scared and I was considering

what my next move should be when music erupted into the room. I looked over to Granny, dancing along to the record she'd just started playing. Fake-Dru's eyes widened. I hurried over to the record player and shut it off.

"Oh, let me have a little fun!" Granny moaned. "After all, she's your enemy, not your friend."

Granny had a point there, but I wasn't sure this was the best way to get Fake-Dru out. I was trying to telepathically tell Granny to knock it off—after all, if she could talk to animals maybe she could read my mind too—but instead she started running around the room switching on every lamp there was.

I turned to Fake-Dru. "Just bad wiring." I tried to sound confident. "It's a really old building."

Granny came and stood next to her and I was afraid of what her next move was going to be. Given the fact that I was the one who had to come up with an explanation for her shenanigans, I secretly wished tasing ghosts was a possibility.

"Stop," I said, exasperated.

"Stop what?" Fake-Dru asked.

"No. I want her out of my house, and since you aren't doing anything, I will." Granny studied her for a moment, "She looks like she's been spray-painted with a bucket full of Pepto-Bismol."

I stifled my laughter as I realized she was right. Fake-Dru had changed into an obnoxious pink tracksuit. Granny gave me a mischievous grin as she plucked up a single strand of Fake-Dru's hair from her shoulder. I shot her a warning look, but she ignored me and began to slowly lift up the white-blonde curl. I could see the sheer joy on Granny's face as she waited for Fake-Dru to notice. She caught it out of the corner of her eye and screamed as she batted her hand at it.

Heather must have still been downstairs working on closing

up the bookstore for the night, because she came bursting through the door with a large bat, no doubt thinking the two of us were killing each other upstairs. She had a ferocious look on her face and stared at us both wild-eyed.

"It's fine, Heather. We're fine," I tried to assure her.

"No, we most certainly are not!" Fake-Dru cried.

"Yes," I said firmly, "she thought she heard someone upstairs and then, of course, you know this old building has some faulty wiring. She just got a little spooked is all."

Heather looked at me curiously for a moment, and then I saw the look of understanding cross her face. She grinned and I knew she had figured out Granny was behind the mystery.

"Yeah, bad wiring." She nodded. "You know, if you're that spooked you can always go back to the Inn."

"No, I'm not leaving." Fake-Dru pouted. "I'll just...I'll just sleep down here on the couch." Oh great. This had just gone from bad to worse. I mentally cursed Granny and gave her the meanest look I could muster.

She just shrugged and muttered. "If she wants to make this hard on herself, I'm up for the challenge. And ghosts don't sleep."

"*Please*," I moaned. "I need to get some sleep tonight!"

"I'll be quiet, I promise. I just... would rather not be alone tonight, that's all." Fake-Dru thought I was talking to her.

I almost felt bad for her. She was visibly scared and she looked a little pathetic standing there. I looked to Heather even though I knew she couldn't do much to help. She offered a sympathetic smile.

The raven cawed loudly, breaking the silence and causing Fake-Dru to jump.

"Oh, mind your business!" Granny scolded. "This is my house and I'll do as I please. I'm not even hurting anyone. Not yet, anyway. I'm just going to have a little fun with someone who truly deserves it. Sure wish I still had my magic, though."

Shoot. Granny's comment reminded me that Fake-Dru being here meant that I wouldn't get to have my lessons with Granny and I was really desperate for them. I had no idea what I was capable of yet, or how any of my magic worked, but there were a lot of things going on in this town and I was certain that magic —any magic at all—would help me find some resolution.

If someone had killed Granny and Trixie, and the two murders were related, that meant no one was really safe. And if my new roommate had anything to do with it, which was a strong possibility, I was in even more danger now than before.

∾

𝓕ake-Dru took the couch, as promised, and I did my best to keep a watchful eye on her all night. Sometime around 4 a.m., amidst the sound of her snoring, Granny told me I really needed to get some sleep and she'd keep an eye on her for me. I dozed off with my hand wrapped tightly around the taser I'd hid under my pillow.

I was only jolted awake twice: once because Fake-Dru was freaking out after she had woken up with the couch moved halfway into the bathroom, and the second time because she'd heard a noise and woken up to a dozen knives levitating in the middle of the room.

I glared at Granny both times. Hadn't she been the one to tell me to get some rest? But she avoided eye contact, the second time muttering something about how they'd only been butter knives. By the time the sun was up, Fake-Dru had already showered and dressed and was on her way out.

"Leaving awfully early, aren't you?" I asked. I'd given up

on sleep myself and was guzzling coffee as she came out of the bathroom.

"Yeah, this place creeps me out," she said. "I didn't sleep well at all last night."

"Me neither," I agreed.

"Oh, wah," Granny said, staring out the window in the kitchen.

"I might go back to the Inn tonight. Until we get things sorted out. I've been calling that lawyer nonstop and he's not answering," Fake-Dru said.

"Trying to get in there to sign the paperwork before I get a chance to?" I asked. "It doesn't matter. You'll still be signing my name. Which is illegal, by the way. And it's only a matter of time before the cops figure out that you're not me. Look, it's just the two of us, so you can drop the act. What's your play here?"

She gave me a blank stare.

"You can't honestly think you'll get away with whatever it is you're trying to get away with," I challenged her, but she remained stoic and we stared at each other in silence for a moment.

"Did I miss a fun night?" a voice came from the other side of the room. I turned to see Trixie standing near the raven's cage.

"Oh!" I couldn't hide my surprise and the utter relief I felt seeing her.

"What?" Fake-Dru questioned me.

I waved my hand. "Nothing. Just remembered something I have to do today."

She eyed me for a moment. "What are you even doing here? You aren't supposed to be here."

"What does that mean?" I asked.

She started to open her mouth and then paused like she was considering something. Instead, she gave a short wave and said goodbye as she headed out the door. As soon as I heard the wooden steps creaking in the hallway, I jumped up from my seat at the kitchen table.

"Trixie!" I exclaimed. "I am *so* happy to see you! I was worried about you!"

"What for?" Granny asked. "She's already been murdered. What's the worst that could happen to her now?"

Trixie giggled but I ignored Granny.

"You just disappeared after the other day and I felt so bad for being rude to you. I was afraid I wouldn't see you again."

"Sorry!" she said. "You seemed to be in a bit of shock and I knew you had a lot to take in. Figured I'd give you a couple days to get used to the idea of ghosts and witches and all." She smiled brightly, twirling one of her blond pigtails around her finger.

"That was sweet, thanks." I walked over to lock the door to the apartment and turned back to them. "Listen, I need to talk to both of you. I've been dying to tell you this." I lowered my voice. "The police chief came by yesterday and Granny, as much as it pains me to say it, you were right."

She turned to me suddenly. I'd definitely gotten her attention.

"He said you were poisoned."

Granny cursed. "I knew it! Oh, someone is going to pay for this. Big time. What else did he say?"

I continued, "He said it was cyanide." I chugged the last of my coffee and grabbed a pair of jeans and an old gray sweatshirt from my suitcase.

"What are you doing?" Trixie asked.

"What she's good at," Granny said, a knowing look in her eyes.

I rolled my eyes. "How would you have any idea if I was good at investigative work or not?"

"Because. You're your father's daughter," she said as if that settled it.

I answered Trixie, "I'm going to follow the fake me today. She's the best lead we have at the moment." I put a gray baseball cap on. It wouldn't hide my distinctive white hair completely, but it was better than nothing.

"Nice disguise," Granny said sarcastically. "So does the chief have any leads at all?"

"He didn't mention anyone specifically. Though I'm sure me and fake me are primary suspects. He just said they'd be interviewing everyone that had motive or opportunity." I sat to put my sneakers on. "Trixie, what do you remember from the night you died? We need to determine if both of your deaths are related at all."

"Not much." She shook her head. "It was dark. I was taking the garbage out back to the alleyway. That's the last thing I remember."

"Okay, if you all are ghosts—" I said.

"If?" Granny interrupted.

"Ugh. *Since* you all are ghosts, don't you immediately show up near your body after you die? Wouldn't you see something? Or do you like go into the light first or whatever?"

"It depends. But if someone kills you, you're not going to know much about it unless you die right away," Trixie answered. "If it takes more than a few minutes, that gives someone plenty of time to sneak up and murder you and run off before you catch a glimpse of them."

I hadn't thought of that. Great. So we had no witnesses and

only one suspect to go on and she only really had motive to kill Granny. Maybe the two weren't linked after all.

"Granny, tell me again what you were doing when you died? Were you alone?"

She nodded, "I do the same thing every Saturday night. After we close up the store and the girls go home, I watch an old western movie and eat a piece of cheesecake before I go to bed."

"It had to have been the cheesecake then," I said. "If you were poisoned with cyanide, then it had to have been that."

Granny nodded.

"Where did it come from?"

"Peaches."

"Peaches?" I was shocked. "That can't be right." True, I'd only met her once, but I couldn't see her being the type to poison anyone.

"Every Saturday I get cheesecake from her," Granny said.

"Did it taste... off?" I asked.

She thought for a moment. "It was a little bitter, I suppose, but it was a new recipe she was trying out. She always tried out her new recipes on me and I was happy being the guinea pig. This one was a cherry coffee concoction. I figured it was too much coffee making it bitter."

"Well, would she have any reason to kill you?" I asked the obvious question.

Granny shook her head. "No, but I don't really know anyone that would. I was beloved."

I scoffed. "Of course you were."

"You know, I would get cheesecake every week, but I'd keep it in the refrigerator down there in the store until I came up for the night. There's all kinds of people in and out of here all day every day," Granny said.

"So it wouldn't have been that hard for someone to tamper with it," I finished for her.

I had seen the refrigerator and Granny was right. It was one of those small ones you might have in a college dorm. It sat below a countertop filled with options for coffee, tea, and water near a quaint sitting area in the corner of the main part of the store.

"I'm going to go out on a limb here and assume you don't have any surveillance cameras for this place?"

Granny shook her head.

"Do you think the same person killed both of us?" Trixie asked.

"I'm not sure." I thought for a moment. "Granny was killed first and my little impostor certainly had a motive if she was after this building and who knows what else. But I don't know how that would have anything to do with you."

"Unless she saw something she wasn't supposed to." I heard a male voice with a British accent. Startled, I looked around the room, but didn't see anyone else.

"Did you hear me?" I heard him again.

"Did anyone else hear that?" I asked aloud.

Granny turned to look at me. "Hear what?"

"That man's voice."

She furrowed her brow. "What did it say?"

Maui jumped onto the coffee table in front of me and cocked his head to one side.

"Are you finally hearing me now, girl? Please say yes. I can't stand another moment only being able to converse with my current company."

"Maui? Is that you talking?"

"You can hear him?" Granny asked, surprised.

"I—I think so, yes." I nodded, dumbfounded.

Trixie squealed in delight.

"Ugh. Please. My ears." Maui visibly winced.

"Oh my gosh! Holy buckets! I can hear you!" I exclaimed.

"That didn't take as long as I thought it would," Granny said.

I stared at Maui. I wasn't sure if I was more surprised by the fact that I could hear him or that he had a British accent.

"I'm glad you can finally get to know the real him now," Granny said. "And I'll tell you, it's a good thing he can't light matches. He's got the personality of an arsonist."

"There's always knocking over candles," Maui replied.

"Why do you have a British accent?" I asked through laughter and tears of disbelief welling in my eyes. I scooped him into my arms.

"How am I supposed to know? I'm just a cat," he responded.

"This is all quite wonderful, really," Granny interrupted. "But if you're going to catch up with that girl you'd better get going. Who knows where she's at by now?" I had completely forgotten my original plan.

"Shoot! That's right." I set Maui on the couch and jumped up, grabbing my purse.

"Listen, Trixie," I said with my hand on the doorknob, "Maui's right. It's possible you saw something you weren't supposed to. While I'm gone, I need you to think. Really hard, okay? Even something you think might not be important. And we'll talk when I get back."

She nodded, and I hoped she could come up with something that might prove to be useful.

CHAPTER 7

$\mathcal{I}$ raced down the stairs and threw open the door leading out into the bookstore. Heather wouldn't be in for at least two more hours, so I locked up behind me on my way out with the extra key she had given me.

I headed toward the corner of Hemlock and Main Street, my eyes darting around like mad in the hopes of spotting Fake-Dru. That's when I saw the bushy-bearded man in the navy shark hat again. He was loitering around in front of an antique store just across the street and seemed caught off-guard by my sudden presence. He turned away and hurried down Main Street toward the Port.

Just as I made the snap decision to continue on with my mission in spite of having a possible stalker, I heard the blip of a police siren behind me. Startled, I turned to see Harper pulling up to the curb.

"Awfully early to be out running around, isn't it?" He leaned out his window. Seeing as how it was probably around 7:30 a.m., wasn't it a little early for him to be coming by for an official interview?

"Uh, yeah. Just couldn't sleep so I thought I'd do some exploring." That wasn't a *total* lie.

"Is that other woman still here? The one I came in with last night?" he asked.

I shook my head. "No, you just missed her." *And now I've lost her too*, I thought.

"Just a minute," he said and rolled up his window. I stood there on the sidewalk, trying my best to eavesdrop without staring at Harper through his closed window. He was speaking into his police radio and after a moment, he turned off his cruiser and opened the door. He stepped out, a paper coffee cup in his hand, and held it out to me.

"White mocha with caramel sauce on top and an extra shot of espresso," he offered.

"That's my favorite. How'd you know?" I asked, taken aback. How could he possibly have known that?

"Lucky guess." He shrugged. *Darn lucky*, I thought.

"So what was that about?" I asked, motioning with my free hand to the radio in his cruiser.

"I was able to run both of your driver's licenses this morning. Thought you might like to know that you are who you claim to be." He winked.

"Thanks for the confirmation," I quipped. "So who is my impostor, anyway?"

"Her name is Tiffany Goldwait. Does that name sound familiar?"

I thought for a moment. "No, it doesn't ring any bells. It isn't familiar at all. Who is she though? Why is she here?"

Harper shook his head. "That's a great question. She's from Florida. No criminal record to speak of." He leaned against his cruiser and rested his hands on his duty belt. "I do intend to find out though. We're pretty swamped with two open murder investigations, but we'll find her. I've got an APB out as well."

I nodded. "Well, she'll probably be coming back here at some point. She left her stuff upstairs. She mentioned this morning that she might go back to whichever one of Cheris Sterling's hotels she was staying in, but she didn't take her suitcase with her when she left this morning."

"Well, that was dumb," Harper muttered. "Here, let me give you my cell number. If you see her, if she shows back up here, get ahold of me, okay?" He handed me a card with his name and contact information on it.

"I will. Thanks," I said.

"I'm sure you hear this all the time, but you have really beautiful eyes. I don't think I've ever seen eyes that color before." He gave me a half smile. "They match that ring on your finger almost exactly."

My cheeks grew hot and I instinctively began fidgeting with the amber stone ring on my middle finger. "The ring was my mother's actually. I used to wear it around my neck on a chain until I was old enough for it to fit my finger." I paused, and forced myself to look up at him. "Anyway, thanks for the compliment."

He studied me for what felt like an eternity.

"I've got your tire," he finally said.

Oh, of course. I'd completely forgotten about my flat tire. "Thanks again for taking care of that for me. I really need to get the car back to the rental company," I said.

"I can get this new one put on and take you to drop it off if you'd like?" he offered.

"Yeah, that would be great." I felt the fluttering in my stomach again at the thought of being alone with him in his car.

~

*A*fter a quick drop off at the rental car company, and Harper teasing me that I'd have to ride in the backseat of his cruiser, we were finally on our way back to Blackwood Bay. Incessant chatter came over his police radio, but after a few minutes he turned it down low.

"Hey, uh, so I wanted to apologize to you for yesterday. The whole situation with that Tiffany Goldwait claiming to be you. She came into the police station and well, it's my job." He seemed nervous.

"No need to apologize," I said, a bit confused as to why he was apologizing in the first place. Just because he'd met me first didn't mean I was the one telling the truth.

"I totally understand you were just doing your job. No hard feelings."

I noticed him giving a toothy grin out of the corner of my eye.

"So, you mentioned yesterday you did some PI work for your dad?" Harper changed the subject.

I nodded. "Yeah. It was kind of an easy decision for me to follow in his footsteps. He was a single dad so I grew up around it. Even when I was little, I remember being so interested in whatever case he was working on. He never showed me the bad stuff, but I do remember going with him on a few stakeouts. He'd make me take a book along and we'd get Chinese and donuts. I loved it so much. I never really took on any cases of my own until the last few years though. Whenever he'd get exceptionally busy, he'd take the big cases for himself and toss me the others. I've only worked a few murder cases, but never any by myself. I mostly just handled the typical stuff—cheating spouses and thieves posing as respectable businessmen."

"It's pretty cool you went into the family business though. I did as well." He smiled.

"Your dad was a police officer too?" I asked.

"Oh, no, he was a carpenter." Harper said straight-faced, looking over his shoulder before changing lanes. I was about to question whether or not he was joking when he said, "I know I mentioned this the other day when we first met, but leaving your career and everything else behind to come here, that's really brave." He eyed me like he was waiting for an explanation.

"There's nothing wrong with wanting a fresh start. Sometimes fate plops something down into your lap that completely changes the course of your life. Maybe inheriting my grandmother's bookstore is that thing for me," I said.

He nodded and gave me a soft smile. We were getting too close to venturing into personal territory and I had no interest in going there with a man I'd only met. I could feel his eyes on me as I stared straight out the windshield at the road ahead.

"So," I said, "how are the cases going anyway? My grandmother's and Trixie's?"

"You know I can't tell you that."

"That's true." I paused. "But, you know, this is a small town that hasn't seen much crime to this degree before. So I've been told, anyway. I imagine the police force is a little overwhelmed. It wouldn't be totally crazy to outsource some of your investigation to, oh, I don't know, a private investigator."

I didn't even know why I said it. The words just tumbled out of my mouth before I had a chance to think it through. I had told myself I was leaving all that behind, and here I was getting caught up in it again and trying to insert myself into an investigation. I told myself if the victims weren't so close to me, if I didn't have a personal stake in it, then I wouldn't have been trying to get involved, but truthfully, I was just placating myself. Being nosy was a part of who I was. It was what had made me so good as a private investigator in the first place.

He laughed. "While you do have a point, hiring a suspect in a murder investigation to help *investigate* said murder is not exactly sound police work."

"Hmm… well, when are you planning to question me so that I can be cleared of any wrongdoing? And why am I a suspect in Trixie's murder? Granny's, I understand I suppose. But I never even met Trixie." *While she was alive, anyway.*

"Because I have a very strong suspicion that they were both killed by the same person. We don't know the cause of death for Trixie yet, but I won't be surprised if it comes back the same as your grandmother's. As to why you, or anyone else, would kill Trixie—that I don't know."

"But I've never even been to this place until two days ago. Both my grandmother and Trixie were killed before I ever even left home," I said.

"So you say." He gave me a sly smile. Was he teasing me? Now really wasn't the time.

"Okay, so when will you interview and clear me then?" There was more bite to my voice than I intended.

"How do you know that's not what I'm doing now?" he asked playfully.

"Are you?"

"Listen, between you and me," his voice took on a serious tone, "I don't actually think you have anything to do with any of it. Your interview and checking your alibi are really just a formality."

That struck me as unusual and I tried to hide my confusion. Granny and her friends knew I was really me and they knew I was innocent because, well, they were either witches or ghosts.

Why would a cop I'd never met until two days ago have the same confidence in me?

Something seemed strange about the whole thing. Was he a witch too? Could men even be witches? All of the witches I'd met so far had let me know, but that didn't mean Harper *wasn't* one either. My head started swimming with confusion, so I decided to just forget it for the moment and ask Granny when I got back to the bookstore.

"Well, are the police in cities hours away from here solid alibis?" I asked.

He gave me a perplexed look.

"I had my car stolen on my way to Blackwood Bay. Then I got a rental and that was stolen too. I called the police both times so there's reports."

"Really?" Harper sounded shocked. "Now that's some bad luck."

"I know. Both times I'd stopped for the night, and when I came out of my hotel room the next morning, my car was gone. I admit, they were pretty cheap hotels, but what are the odds?"

"Wow. That's unbelievable." Harper looked thoughtful. "Have you noticed anyone following you?" I hadn't even considered that I had been followed all the way from my home in Nevada until that moment. The image of the man in the navy shark hat popped into my head. I told Harper that I'd seen a man a couple of times since I'd arrived in town, but it could just be coincidence.

"If you see him near you or the bookstore again, call me, all right?" Harper clenched his jaw, but the hard look on his face passed quickly and he spoke in a cheerful tone. "To answer your question, yes the police are about the best alibi you can get."

"Good." I nodded.

"How are you settling in?" Harper changed the subject.

You mean besides the ghosts and talking animals keeping me up all hours of the night? "Quite well, thanks. Aside from having a new roommate last night," I said.

"I'm sorry about that." He looked a little sheepish. "Until we were able to prove anything, we had to give her the same fair treatment we gave you."

"I know. Why did you think I was the one telling the truth though?" I asked. I was used to solid police work and investigators that were suspicious of everything. This was too easy and instead of being a relief, it was a little unsettling.

"Ah, well," he paused to take a sip of his coffee before carefully setting it back down in the cup holder, "I can't *say* that I do. I was a big city detective up until a month ago. But this is a small town with a lot of old faces. There's plenty of folks around here who knew your grandmother and both of your parents. Including the chief. From what I hear, you're the spitting image of your mother, by the way."

Wow. I was hit with a powerful wave of emotion. I'd never even met any of these people, but it seemed like I didn't just have a grandmother here, but something akin to a family that I never even knew about.

"Besides, if I ran you out of town, Peaches would do the same to me," he joked. "I was in yesterday sometime after you left and she was raving on and on about you."

I felt a bit of guilt rise up in me for thinking she could've possibly been the one to hurt Granny.

"So how does your wife like it here?" I had to ask. I kind of hated myself for it, but I had to know if he was single.

"No wife. It's just me."

"So, you're kind of a lone wolf?" I realized that I'd just inadvertently made a pun using his first name and felt my cheeks flush. Fortunately, he laughed.

"Yeah, you might say I am. No significant other for you either?" he asked, casually taking a drink of his coffee.

This was my moment. I didn't know if he was attracted to me or if he was just being friendly to another new face in town, but if Harper *was* interested in me, this was my opportunity to warn him that I'd just had my heart broken and I was still trying to pick up the pieces. It wouldn't be smart for either of us for him to try to get involved with me. We approached a red stoplight and I could feel his eyes studying me. Suddenly I couldn't find words—just a lump in my throat.

I decided to buy some time and lifted my coffee cup toward my mouth but the paper was just slick enough, and my hands just shaky enough, that I felt it slide from my grip. I looked down and watched it begin to fall, almost as if in slow motion. *No, please, no. Do not spill hot coffee all over my lap and this gorgeous policeman's car,* I pleaded, dread filling my entire body.

And then, the cup froze in place. Just suspended in the air right there above my lap. I blinked a couple of times. Yes, still just hanging there as if placed on an imaginary table. My hand shook as I reached out to grab it. What had just happened? Had I just done that with my mind? I looked at Harper, but he didn't seem to notice anything out of the ordinary had just occurred, checking his side mirror as he switched lanes.

I managed to shake my head, trying to force the words to come. "Um, No. No significant other for me either," I said, my voice a bit unsteady as I secured the coffee cup in both of my hands. My heart felt like it was going to pound right out of my chest.

I glanced over at Harper again and he gave me a strange smile in return. I suddenly had the sneaking suspicion that this man was just as strange as he was handsome.

CHAPTER 8

I didn't make it back to the bookstore until close to 9:30 a.m. and found Heather already sitting on a stool behind the register. She looked up from her book when I came in.

"Where have you been off to so early again this morning?" She shoved a purple bookmark in to keep her place and shut the book. *Book of Spells and Incantations, 100th Edition.* I made a mental note that I probably needed to read that one myself.

"By the way, that woman showed up this morning just as I was opening up. She wanted to get her suitcase and then she took off," Heather said.

"She did?" I asked. Great. Now she really was in the wind. I decided to shoot Harper a quick text to let him know.

He responded almost immediately.

Don't worry. We'll find her. Stay safe.

Heather caught me smiling at my phone and made a little noise with her tongue. "Where did you say you were this morning?"

"Well, I was going to follow the fake me this morning, but I got... sidetracked."

Heather raised her eyebrows.

"That cop from yesterday—"

"The hot one?" she cut me off.

I nodded. "He showed up this morning and took me to return my rental car."

Heather gave a knowing smile. "You're going to have to tell me a lot more than that." She opened a plastic bag and popped a cherry into her mouth, sliding the bag to the middle of the counter between us. I grabbed one and ate it slowly as I gathered my thoughts.

"Well, I think he just wanted to get some intel on me."

Heather scoffed, popped a cherry pit out of her mouth, and placed it on a napkin on the counter. "He could've done that at the station. That's where *I* have to go. He likes you. I can tell."

"Can men be witches too?" I asked.

"No." Heather shook her head. So Harper wasn't a witch, but there was definitely something different about him. I just wasn't sure what yet.

I grabbed another cherry and was reminded of the cherry coffee cheesecake Granny had mentioned. I still felt guilty thinking Peaches might've been involved, but it *was* her cheesecake that was poisoned. I knew the police wouldn't have tested it. They assumed an old lady died of natural causes, so the cheesecake was long gone, rotted away in a dump somewhere, before they figured out she'd been poisoned. I hadn't mentioned it to Harper because, well, I received that bit of information from a ghost. I decided to run it past Heather to see what she thought, after all, she knew both Granny and Peaches better than I did.

"Hey, so Granny said that her last meal, so to speak, was

cheesecake from Peaches' place. I hate to even bring it up, but since we know she was poisoned…" I trailed off. I wasn't sure what I was asking exactly and I hoped Heather would fill in the blanks.

She looked deep in thought for a moment. "I mean, I know she likes to let Granny try out her new recipes, and she's had some real doozies before, but nothing *that* bad," Heather joked.

"So you trust her then? You don't think she's capable of something like that?"

Heather shook her head. "No, I don't. I mean, I know she wanted Granny to sell her this place—"

"She did?" I was surprised. Neither one of them had mentioned that.

"Yeah, from what I hear she's been interested in it for quite some time. I guess she wanted to keep it as a bookstore but add a lighter version of her café. Just coffee, espresso, and baked goods." Heather popped another cherry into her mouth. "But that's certainly no reason to murder somebody, right?" she asked. It was actually a very good reason to murder somebody and I'd seen people kill for a lot less.

Heather continued, "Anyway, how would she finally convince Granny to sell it to her if Granny was dead. It doesn't make any sense."

"It makes a lot of sense," I started. I had only known Heather for a couple of days and I wasn't sure I could trust her completely yet. I mean, she had a solid relationship with Peaches and I was basically a stranger. Still, I needed to work through this with someone that wasn't directly involved, i.e., a murder victim or a cop, so she would have to do.

"Think about it. It would be much easier to convince someone to sell it if they had no real stake in the place. Granny owned this place for what, sixty years? Of course she wouldn't sell it. But a newcomer with no experience and no ties to this town other than the dead grandmother they never even met? Might be a whole lot easier to convince them to sell."

Heather's eyebrows were raised and I could tell I'd piqued her curiosity. "I don't know. That's awfully devious."

"So is murder," I said. "What about Dorothy?" I remembered the comment Peaches had made about Dorothy wanting to be the 'queen bee.'

"What about her?" Heather hopped off her stool and went to the small sink along the wall to wash her hands.

"I don't know. She said her and Granny were close, but did you ever get the sense there was any rivalry between them?"

Heather thought for a moment while she dried her hands on a paper towel, "Now that you mention it," she tossed the paper towel into the trash bin and headed back toward me, "they did squabble quite a bit. Granny was definitely in charge around here, and not just because her building is our home base. Dorothy, as I'm sure you could tell even from one encounter with her, has a very... demanding presence. And she's not one to mince words if she disagrees with you. Granny had an equally demanding presence though, even more so really. They sometimes disagreed on things. Me, for one."

"You?" I asked.

She nodded. "When I first came here, Granny was quick to welcome me into our coven with open arms. Dorothy kept me at arm's length. I think she really only warmed up to me these last few months. Still, I sometimes question whether she actually likes or just tolerates me." Heather gave a nervous laugh. I had no indication that things had ever been tense between her and Dorothy—they seemed friendly to each other when I'd seen them together—but I was also having the craziest day of my life that day, so it's possible I missed something.

"I didn't realize you were new here. Every other witch I've met seems to have lived here their whole life. I guess I just assumed you had as well. How long have you been here then?" I asked.

"Two years next month." She smiled and glanced at her watch. "Well, I'd better go. I told Chief Carver I'd be in first thing this morning and I'm already late."

I started to panic. She was leaving me alone here?

She turned when she reached the door. "Oh, don't worry. It's usually pretty slow on mid-weekday mornings. If you need help, I'm sure Granny can offer some assistance. Or Trixie? Is she still... around?" she glanced around the bookstore.

"Sometimes. I've seen her upstairs."

Heather nodded. "I'll try to hurry. Oh, by the way, tonight is our coven meeting. Nine o'clock sharp."

"I'll be here," I said. As if I really had a choice.

I looked around the store. For the first time since I'd arrived, I was completely alone. The silence was almost deafening. I decided now was as good a time as any to explore a little bit. After all, this place was mine now. I should probably learn what we were selling exactly and where things were located. I started with the bookshelves. They were organized by special topic.

As I meandered up and down the rows of books, my mind began to wander as I thought about my strange experience at breakfast. Had I really levitated that coffee cup with my mind? I mean, I was a witch after all. Did that mean I could use magic to move things without touching them? If so, my life was just about to get a whole lot lazier.

I decided to do a little experimenting. I did a quick scan of the windows within view of my spot behind a middle row of bookshelves. All clear. I picked out a random book on the shelf, a glossy leather bound with intricate filigree on its spine. *Okay, book, come to me,* I thought. It didn't budge. Hmm... okay, I should've known this was going to be more complicated than that.

I thought about what was happening right before I suspended the coffee cup in midair. I was nervous, uncomfortable, and would've been mortified to spill an entire cup of hot coffee all over myself and Harper's cruiser. My cheeks flushed just thinking about it. Okay, so strong emotion? Is that what I needed to make this work? I tried to tap into those feelings that I had experienced earlier and willed the book to move again but it still didn't budge.

"What's happening here? Did you have a stroke?" Granny's voice came from behind me and I jumped. "You're just standing there staring. Are you all right?"

"Yes, I'm trying to make this book come to me. This morning, I dropped a coffee cup and I was able to stop it from spilling everywhere. At least I think I did it. It was levitating. I think I can move things with my mind," I said.

She rolled her eyes at me. "You mean when you were off on your hot date instead of trying to track down my killer?"

"Granny, I was gathering information and I had to return my rental car," I responded. "Listen, I've been talking to people and I have quite a list of possible suspects already. Talking to that cop this morning was really helpful."

"Mmhmm... I'm sure it was. A list of suspects isn't going to do much if you can't narrow it down though, now is it?"

I groaned. "Granny, I'm trying. I really am. I can't just go running around town interrogating everyone. That's the last thing that works. Especially for someone that isn't even in law enforcement, by the way. You do realize people don't have to tell me squat, right? I have to pull information out of them carefully. Talk to their friends and their enemies. It's a process."

She studied me for a moment. "Okay," she said, seeming to drop it for the time being. "Now, about that moving things with your mind business. Are you holding your magic like I taught you?"

"Yes, of course." Actually, no. I'd forgotten about that part. I turned my back to her. "Now please be quiet so I can concentrate."

I stared at the book again, holding my magic was difficult as it wasn't something that felt natural. Kind of like holding your body in a push-up position. The longer you do it the harder it gets. Just as I was about to give up, the book started to wiggle out from its spot. I concentrated harder, feeling my jaw tense as I clenched my teeth, and I envisioned what I wanted the book to do. It slid out easily then, and made its way toward me, albeit wobbly, until it hovered a few feet from my face.

"I did it," I whispered.

"You did!" Granny exclaimed. "Keep going! The more you practice the easier it gets. Just like riding a bike."

I turned the book on its back then, just to see if I could do it.

"Hello?" I heard a voice come from the front of the store. I really needed to buy that bell. The book instantly dropped to the floor with a loud thud.

"Careful!" Granny scolded.

"Um… yes, coming!" I called out, picking up the book and shoving it back into the bookshelf. I hurried to the storefront, smoothing down my hair and desperately hoping the woman hadn't seen anything. She had her back to me when I approached and even though I'd only met her once before, I immediately recognized her perfectly-fitted outfit and dark pixie cut. Her perfume was already invading the air in the room, over-powering the smell of burning incense.

Something told me she was not the type to frequent a store like this, and if she wasn't a local, I would've assumed she was lost.

"Hi Cheris." I smiled. "How can I help you?"

She removed her large black sunglasses and I noticed that when she offered me a polite smile, there was nothing in her eyes. She reminded me a bit of an old Hollywood movie star in her black shift dress and heels, large pearls hugging her neck.

"I just thought I'd stop in and see how things were going? Did you get that whole mess sorted out with the girl from my hotel?"

Granny stood behind her, arms crossed and a scowl on her face.

"Yes, Sergeant Harper stopped by this morning." I didn't want to give her any more information than necessary.

"Ah," she nodded, "well, I'm sure it's nice to have that headache over with." She gave a small laugh. "So what are your plans for this place now that that's done and over with?"

"She's fishing," Granny said. "She's a snake but she's always fishing."

"Well," I addressed Cheris as she looked around the book-store, "I guess hire a new employee to lighten Heather's work-load. After that, I'm not really sure." It was true.

"So you plan on staying then? Running this place yourself?" She was still looking around.

"That's the plan," I responded, curious as to what she was really doing there. I had a feeling she didn't actually care how well I was settling in.

"Well, it's a fine piece of property, you know." She paused. "You could sell it for a fair amount." She turned back to me then and gave her signature tight smile. "You're still so young. Don't you have dreams and aspirations? To travel the world? Buy yourself a nice new car? Maybe a cute little cottage on the beach somewhere? Doesn't that sound lovely?"

I had to admit it did.

"You're much too young to be strapped down to this old place. Have you ever even run a business before, dear?"

"There it is!" Granny's voice was angry. "I knew she'd do this! That hag! Tell her she's a hag!" I had to keep myself from smiling.

"No, I haven't. But I'm really excited for this new adventure," I said, choosing to ignore Granny's efforts to get me to insult the woman.

"Hmm," she said with a nod. "What if I offered you an above-market price for this place?"

"You? Why?" I was stunned. Cheris was a hotel owner, not a bookstore owner.

Granny grumbled but the only thing I could make out besides a few choice curse words was 'snake.'

"As I'm sure you've heard, I own the hospitality market in this town. A few bed and breakfasts, a host of inns, and a couple of old hotels that I've carefully restored. People come here for the charm of this place and when they do so, they want the full experience. In order to have that, they stay in one of my properties. Some of my most celebrated and popular establishments are the oldest buildings in town." Now I could see where this was going. She continued, "People like the historical charm, but they also love the rumors that come along with it."

"Rumors?" I interrupted.

She gave a short laugh. "Yes, rumors of seeing ghosts. That the buildings are haunted. People say they hear things in the night. See things even. It's all quite silly but it makes me a fortune."

"You don't believe in ghosts?" I asked.

She waved her hand and scoffed. "No, I don't, certainly." She laughed. "But if it keeps bringing in the money, then I'm happy to give the people what they want." Her posture changed then, a serious look on her face. "This building that we're standing in is the oldest in this town. It has a great history and my guests would *love* it. I tried for years to get your grandmother to sell it to me, but she was so stubborn that woman. She didn't really have much else, so I suppose it makes a bit of sense."

Granny cursed her again.

"But you, you have no ties to this place. You're young and you can do absolutely anything you want." She leaned in as if she was about to tell me a secret. I noticed her spot the napkin filled with cherry pits on the counter and I felt a surge of embarrassment that I'd forgotten to throw them away. "I will give you three million dollars cash—right now—if you agree to sign the deed over to me." Did I hear that right? Three million?!

"Don't you dare! Don't you even consider it!" Granny's voice was trembling with anger.

"Listen," Cheris gave my hand a quick pat, "you think about it and I'll catch up with you in the next day or two. All right? Talk to your father. He's a smart man. This is a wonderful offer and an opportunity for you to start your life over *right*." She put her sunglasses on and headed for the door.

"Witch!" Granny yelled as the door banged closed.

"I know I'm new at this, but I don't think you're supposed to use that as a derogatory term," I said.

"Ohhh, that woman! I should've warned you she'd come slithering around now that I'm dead."

"Oh, and dear?" Cheris was back, just her head poking through a crack in the door.

"You have some kind of an animal, yes? A cat perhaps?" she asked, her eyes peeking over the top of her sunglasses.

"How did you know?"

"I can see the hair on your shirt. Anyway, you might want to be sure to dispose of those cherry pits properly. In a sealed bag and straight into the dumpster out back."

"Why?"

"Because cherry pits are poisonous, dear. In fact, just a couple of them can kill a person. Wouldn't want anything to happen to your darling little kitty cat." She smiled and with that, she was gone.

CHAPTER 9

"*I*s that true?" I turned to Granny.

"I have no idea." She shrugged. "That woman is slicker than owl crap, but I'm not sure why she'd lie about something like that."

I pulled my cell phone out of my purse and set to work searching the internet.

"Yes, it *is* true." I looked at Granny but I could tell she didn't understand why that mattered much.

"Granny, what if this is how you were poisoned?"

"What?" Trixie appeared behind me and I jumped.

"Listen, you two. Granny ate a piece of cherry coffee cheesecake, right? And you said it tasted a little bitter but you thought it was because of the coffee?" I asked Granny.

She nodded.

"What if it was from cherry pits? Apparently, your body turns them into cyanide if they're chewed or ground up. Some people have reported them as having a bitter taste. But, as Cheris said, it only takes a few to kill someone and you're a tiny woman anyways."

"But wouldn't she notice she was eating big old cherry pits?" Trixie asked.

"No, they would've been ground up into a powder or something and mixed in." I didn't have the heart to reply sarcastically to her at that point. "Trixie, tell us what you were doing right before you went outside the night you died."

She thought for what seemed like an eternity. "I put on my shoes and a sweater 'cause I thought it might be a little cold that time of night."

"Before that," I said.

"Went to the bathroom."

"Before that."

"I paused the movie I was watching. I'd seen it lots of times but it's one of my favorites—"

"Hell's bells! You know, you're sweet, but you are twelve short of a dozen, girl," Granny said what we both were thinking.

"I thought there was only twelve in a dozen?" Trixie looked baffled.

"Okay, what time did you eat dinner?" I decided to try a different tactic.

Trixie thought for a moment. "About seven thirty or so, I think."

"Okay, so what did you eat? Did you prepare the food yourself? Or did you buy it… somewhere?" I asked. I didn't want to mention Peaches but I was really freaking out that she might've been the one who poisoned Granny. In order for the ground cherry pits to be in the cheesecake, it would've required that they be baked in. Which meant that whoever baked the cheesecake—Peaches—was the most likely suspect.

She nodded. "It was just a TV dinner."

"Hmm… okay. Then what did you do? You said you

watched a movie. Did you eat or drink anything during that time?" I knew I was onto something here.

"Oh!" she exclaimed. "Yes."

Granny and I waited, but her patience ran out before mine did and she threw her arms up in exasperation. "What! What was it?"

"I had a cup of tea. I do every night before bed. Helps me sleep." She giggled.

"Well, this time it helped you sleep forever," Granny muttered.

"Okay," I rolled my eyes at Granny's quip, "did you get it from someone else?"

"Nope. Same one I always drink."

"Does anyone else have a key to your house? Or did you have any visitors since Granny died?" I asked.

Trixie stared up at the ceiling for a few moments and Granny finally answered for her, "It doesn't matter. Everyone knew she hid her spare key under a potted plant on her front porch. It's a wonder she lived as long as she did, really."

"Granny!" I scolded her before addressing Trixie. "Did the tea taste strange at all?"

"She wouldn't know," Granny interrupted, "because she puts a pound of sugar in her tea."

"Yeah, it didn't taste weird really. Just sweet. Does that help?" Trixie asked.

"Yes, it does."

"No," Granny said at the same time.

"It helps, Trixie. I'm thinking maybe someone replaced one of your regular tea bags with one that was poisoned. I'm guessing that the ME will find out that you were poisoned the same way Granny was." She looked all kinds of confused, so I changed the subject.

"Did you get a chance to think about if there was anything you might've seen that you weren't supposed to?"

She gave me a blank stare.

"Remember when I asked you this morning to do that? Granny had her cheesecake down here in that refrigerator the day she died." I pointed to the refrigerator in the corner. "Did you see anyone over there that shouldn't have been?" I asked.

Peaches was our most obvious suspect, but I was having a really hard time accepting it. She had been so sweet to me and I just couldn't wrap my mind around the possibility that she would've done something so terrible. I kept looking for another solution.

Trixie shook her head.

"Granny, how was your relationship with Peaches?" I asked.

"Good. Why?"

"Because if this is how you were poisoned…" I trailed off.

"I told you—a lot of people were in and out of here that day."

"Right, but I don't think you can just sprinkle cyanide onto the top of food. I'm guessing the cherry pits were *in* the cheesecake somehow. Which means whoever made it…"

Granny looked hurt. "She wouldn't do that. She would never."

"Granny, I really like her too, but I'm just trying to look at the facts. They're hard to ignore."

She didn't say anything.

"Also, something Heather said this morning got me thinking." I recalled to Granny how she'd mentioned that Peaches wanted to buy Granny's store. It seemed to be a hot commodity in this town. And quite possibly something someone would kill for.

"It wasn't really like that." Granny sounded annoyed.

"Peaches told me she wanted to bring her touch to this place and offer some baked goods and coffee. I told her I wasn't interested in selling. She said I was getting old and it would be getting more difficult for me to keep up with this place. I told her that's what I had my staff for and she was no spring chicken herself. And that was the end of it."

"Was she angry about it?" I asked.

Granny shrugged. "If she was, she seemed to get over it pretty quickly."

"What about Dorothy? How was your relationship with her?"

"Good. Fine," she said curtly.

Trixie giggled. "They got along like cats and dogs."

Granny waved her hand dismissively. "We were like sisters. Sisters argue. We didn't always see eye-to-eye, but..." She shrugged.

"And Heather? How well do you really know her? She said she's only been here a couple of years."

"Are you going to accuse every single one of my friends?" Granny asked.

Interesting. Either Granny had a hard time admitting the truth about her relationships, or I was being fed inaccurate information from nearly every source. The truth was, as much as I liked everyone, that I didn't know any of them and I didn't know who I could trust. Even Harper gave me a bit of pause. As it stood, I could trust three beings: two ghosts and one talking cat.

"Yes, I am. Because someone murdered you. Someone poisoned you. And then they did the same thing to Trixie. At least I think. That's not a random act by some stranger. It's personal."

Granny adjusted her glasses and crossed her arms over her

chest. "Okay, what about Cheris then? She was the one in here telling you about the cherry pits. Seems like she was baiting you to me," Granny countered. She wasn't entirely wrong either. "She's been after this place for years. Killing me and buying from you would've been her best bet."

"But how did she know I existed in the first place?" I asked.

"Everyone around here knows. It's no secret."

"What if she's the one who paid the lawyer off to draft up fake documentation?" Maui's voice came from the bottom of the staircase. I hadn't heard him creep in, but his theory actually made a lot of sense.

"What about my impostor though? What's her role in all of this?" I asked.

Maui purred. "Perhaps she wants to take this place and sell it. Perhaps she knows how much it's worth. Though that would certainly be a step up in the identity theft game." He licked his single white paw.

"So we currently have three possible suspects, all of whom want this building," I said.

"Which makes you, if you're unwilling to sell, the next target," Maui finished for me and I felt a shiver run up my spine.

CHAPTER 10

*I*t was my first official coven meeting and to say I was overwhelmed would be a massive underestimation.

The witches started pouring in at promptly nine o'clock and I was awash in a sea of *oohs* and *ahhs* and hugs. Some of them even cried as they told me how happy they were to meet me and how close they'd been with my mother. Of all the things I'd experienced so far in Blackwood Bay, that was the most surreal.

I had been calling both my dad and Mitch Powders all day and it was going straight to voicemail for both. I really wanted to talk to my dad, but instead I hovered by the Potluck-style food table for a while, trying to regain my bearings as I looked for familiar faces.

Dorothy and Minnie came strolling in a few minutes late, a look of agitation on Dorothy's face as Minnie hurried behind her. Dorothy approached first while Minnie went to place a wrapped platter with the rest of the food.

"Hello, sweetheart." She gave me a warm smile and pulled me in for a hug. "Do *not* eat the chimichangas," she whispered.

"Minnie made them." She pulled back just as Minnie approached.

"Oh, Dru! It's so nice to see you again!" Minnie threw her arms around me. "Make sure you try one of my chimichangas. They're chicken. I bet they're just delicious." She beamed. Dorothy mouthed 'no' and shook her head vigorously.

"Thanks, Minnie." I offered her a polite smile and she sauntered away.

"Minnie tries to use magic when she cooks," Dorothy leaned in and explained. "I say tries because it's always disastrous in some way but she just keeps on trying. I do admire her tenacity, but I certainly won't let you fall victim to it." She eyed me for a moment. "Are you doing okay, dear?"

"Yeah, it's just a little overwhelming. All these new faces and everyone talking about my mother."

Dorothy squeezed my shoulder. "I'm sure it is. We can be a boisterous, obnoxious bunch, but we really are a family. Everyone here is looking forward to seeing you come into your own and we're happy to help in any way we can."

I nodded, thankful to have so many people who cared about me that I'd never even met before—and feeling guilty for having suspicions about any of them.

"We should probably get started," Dorothy said and headed toward the crowd of women sprawled out in the sitting area: some on the furniture, some on folding chairs, and some huddled on the blue-green carpet. I noticed Maui, who had followed me downstairs from the apartment, perched on the front counter, surveying the group before him.

"Ladies, ladies!" Dorothy raised her voice and the chattering died down. She raised her right hand with a pointed finger and spun around the room. Was she doing the hokey-pokey?

"A cloaking spell. From the outside, it will appear as though

we're just a group of women sitting around with books in our
hands," she explained as she motioned for me to come over. "I
know you've all met Dru, and I know everyone has welcomed
her with open arms. Remember that she's only just learned she's
a witch, so we must take her under our wing and help her grow
into her magic." I heard murmurs of agreement and spotted
Peaches, Astra, and Electra crammed together on folding chairs
behind the couch. I gave a little wave as they smiled at me.

"Are Granny and Trixie joining us this evening?" a woman
asked.

Woman? Witch? What was I supposed to call them—us? I
wasn't sure yet. She was a slight woman with hair dyed a
vibrant shade of red. It was a bit disheveled and, paired with her
oversized white button up shirt and black leggings, she looked
like she'd been ready to turn in for the night when she suddenly
remembered she had somewhere to be.

She spoke with a British accent. "I'm Tilly, by the way."
She smiled.

I looked around the bookstore but didn't see either Granny
or Trixie. "No, I don't think so. At least they aren't here at the
moment. Am I the only one who can see ghosts?"

"It's a very rare power to have." Dorothy said.

"How're the cases going? Have y'all heard anything?"
Peaches piped up.

"Chief Carver came in last night and told us that Granny
was poisoned," I said. My words were met with a collective
gasp.

"Oh, I bet she's just havin' a dyin' duck fit," Peaches said. I
wondered if she really didn't know Granny died from eating her
cheesecake or if she was just a really good actress.

"Have you heard anything about Trixie?" Electra piped up.

I shook my head. It was true; I hadn't. I only had suspicions.

"Hmm... two witches from the same coven dead in a matter of a few weeks," a voice came from the floor. She reminded me of what one might think a new-aged witch looked like. Her caramel-colored hair had a natural wave to it, and her cream peasant dress created the perfect backdrop for her silver and turquoise jewelry and sun-kissed skin. I noticed she was barefoot and saw a pair of worn leather sandals lying on the floor next to her.

"Don't say it, Eve. Don't even say it," Dorothy warned.

"Why not? I can't be the only one thinking it." Eve's voice had a melodic tone when she spoke and I imagined if she had children, they probably enjoyed her reading them bedtime stories.

"What's she talking about?" Minnie had a worried look on her face as she took a seat next to Tilly on the couch.

Tilly reached out and patted Minnie's hand on her lap.

Eve adjusted the thick silver cuff on her forearm. "Come on, Dorothy. Not talking about it won't change anything."

I felt awkward standing in front of everyone with Dorothy and scanned the room for a seat I could escape to. Unless I wanted to plop down right there on the floor, I was out of luck. Maui must've sensed my discomfort, because suddenly he was at my side, circling through my legs.

"It really is what we're all thinking," Astra spoke up. Dorothy hung her head and exhaled.

"Can someone please tell me what you're all talking about?" I asked.

"Yes, goodness. Get on with it," Maui said as I scooped him into my arms.

"Heather, dear, are you all right with us discussing this?" Tilly turned to Heather, who stood near the back of the group, a deer-caught-in-the-headlights look on her face.

"Witch hunters?" Minnie gasped. "Is that what you're talking about?" She looked at Tilly who gave her a little nod.

"Witch hunters?" I asked.

"Brilliant. As if we didn't have enough to worry about already," Maui said.

"I can tell her." Heather walked forward and Peaches stood to offer her seat.

"I told you earlier today that I came here almost two years ago. But I didn't tell you why," she addressed me directly. Yeah, I'd been wondering about that.

"Most witches stay with covens they're born into. Not always of course, but generally. And I would've too, but..." I really didn't like where I thought this was heading.

Peaches put a supportive arm around Heather's shoulders.

"We were a small coven, only ten of us or so. Basically in the middle of nowhere in a small town in Vermont. We lived a comfortable existence. No one knew what we were and no one really bothered us. Until..." her voice caught. "Until one night just before Halloween. We were set to have our usual coven meeting, but I was running late. I tried calling to let them know but no one was answering their phones. When I finally arrived, almost thirty minutes late, it was... it was a terrible scene." She lowered her head and wiped under her eyes as Peaches squeezed her shoulders.

Heather looked back up at me, tears streaming down her cheeks. "They were all dead. I saw a man through the window. I had seen him lurking around for a few weeks and I had my suspicions that he was a witch hunter, but everyone said I was being paranoid. I should've done something when I saw him that night, but I was in shock and too scared. So I ran. I'd visited this place before and I knew, of all the covens, this was probably the safest. With your Granny here and all. So I came here."

"Wow, Heather, I'm so sorry." I didn't really know what to say. I wanted to ask her how a human man could go in and kill a whole group of magical witches, but it didn't feel appropriate when I saw the looks of sympathy on the faces around the room. Besides, what did I know about any of this stuff? Maybe witch hunters weren't regular humans either. I'd have to ask someone about it at a more appropriate time, I decided.

"Our kind has been battling witch hunters since the beginning. There's not many left, but they're a persistent bunch. Usually we can snuff them out and deal with them before anyone gets hurt, but not always," Dorothy explained.

"Well, witch hunters are bothersome, of course, but that's not what I was referring to," Eve broke in. I noticed a levitating cupcake making its way to her. It stopped in her outstretched hand and she smiled as she began peeling back the paper liner.

Heather sniffled. "My entire coven being murdered is a bit worse than bothersome." She had an edge to her voice.

"Yes, of course it is, darlin'." Peaches smoothed her hand over Heather's hair and shot a glare at the back of Eve's head.

"And what exactly are you referring to then, Eve?" Dorothy said curtly.

"Dark witches," Eve said matter-of-factly before licking a bit of pink frosting from the side of her cupcake. A collective gasp burst into the room, followed by a myriad of competing voices filled with urgency.

"Dark witches?" Dorothy raised her voice. "Certainly not."

"What are dark witches?" I asked. Granny had mentioned them on that first night, but she hadn't elaborated.

"Dark witches," Tilly started, "are evil. Simply put. They don't use their magic for good. They hide from us, mostly.

Because they use their magic for evil purposes, it's not quite as strong as ours—"

"Unless…" Eve interrupted.

"Unless," Tilly continued, "they steal it."

"Steal it?" I didn't understand.

"Basically, a witch can steal another witch's magical energy," Tilly said.

"By killing the first witch and reciting a very specific incantation," Eve said.

"Okay, wait. I don't understand—" I started.

"It hasn't happened for centuries. But one witch can steal another witch's magic for herself. Only if the first witch doesn't have an heir to pass her magic onto, though. If I were a dark witch, I could kill Dorothy, for example," a smirk crossed her face, "since she has no one to inherit her magic, and recite an incantation that would let me take her magic for myself. A dark witch could become incredibly powerful if she targeted the right witches as her victims. It would be pretty catastrophic for our kind too," Eve finished and took a bite out of her cupcake. It was a little disturbing how unbothered she was talking about it.

"I really don't think that's what's going on here," Dorothy said. "It hasn't happened in so long—"

"What about children?" I asked, suddenly horrified at the thought of witch hunters and dark witches going after innocent children.

Tilly shook her head. "Even dark witches won't hurt a child. It's just not in our DNA. Besides, children possess very little magical energy, even if they've inherited from a passing ancestor. They don't really come into their magic until adulthood. As for witch hunters, most of them aren't wicked enough but we put extra protection in place for our children just in case."

"Like what? A spell or something?" I asked.

"A specific protection spell is just one way. It's one of the things your Granny did for you before your daddy took you away," Peaches said. Granny had *not* told me that little bit of information. Why was she keeping things from me?

"Would that keep me from knowing I was a witch? From being aware of my powers?" I asked.

"No," a few women answered, shaking their heads, but no one offered me any further explanation. I was confused.

Granny hadn't mentioned putting any kind of spell on me. She'd just said that my father had to take me away to keep me safe. Safe from what though? Dark witches? Witch hunters? And did they have something to do with what happened to my mother? I needed to know, and I was about to ask, but I realized that I wanted to have that conversation with my father and my grandmother. Not a room full of people I'd just met.

"So, you all think either a witch hunter or a dark witch is behind this?" I asked instead.

There was some incomprehensible chatter as everyone looked around the room nervously at each other.

"Dru has some suspicions," Heather said over the noise in the room. What was she doing? She crossed the room, stopping at the table to grab a chimichanga, and stood next to me, all but bumping Dorothy out of the way. I was about to whisper to her that she really shouldn't eat that, but Minnie interrupted.

"Suspicions?" Minnie asked.

"No, I don't. I just—" this was not the time or the place or the group to discuss any of this with.

"Yes, she was asking me questions this morning about a few of you," Heather turned to me. "Tell them."

"What an absolute twit this one is!" Maui exclaimed, jumping from my arms. I noticed a grin forming on Eve's face and wondered if she could hear him too.

Okay, why was she throwing me under the bus like that? I thought she was my friend.

"Heather." *Shut it*, I tried to tell her with my eyes, but she didn't seem to get the message. Did she really not see why this was a bad idea?

"Go on. Tell them what Granny told you."

I sighed. All right, here goes.

"It's just that, well, like I said earlier. Granny was poisoned." I paused.

"Yes?" Tilly prodded.

"And she said she died while she was eating a piece of cheesecake." Everyone stared at me. *Please don't make me say it.*

"This isn't going to go well at all." Maui purred, curling up in Eve's lap.

"She said she got it from Peaches," I said barely above a whisper. I heard a few gasps, but I lowered my eyes.

"She also said that there were *a lot* of people in and out of here all day so anyone could have tampered with it," I finished. I was afraid to look at Peaches but something willed me to. I was expecting a look of anger, maybe reddened cheeks and a grimace. Instead, her eyes were watery and I saw her lip tremble. Astra had her hand on Peaches' forearm and Electra stood next to her mother solicitously.

"Are you saying my cheesecake killed Granny?" Peaches choked out.

"I'm purely speculating, but I think it might've. Yes," I said. Peaches put her face in her hands and I saw her shoulders heave. Fantastic, I'm a monster.

"Mama did *not* poison Granny!" Astra shot daggers at me with her eyes.

"I didn't say she did," I stuttered. Although, to be fair, I did suspect her.

"She would never! She loved her!" Electra was just as angry as her sister.

"Girls, please calm down. Dru isn't accusing anyone." Dorothy stepped in front of me.

"She asked me about your relationship too, Dorothy," Heather said. What in the world? What was she doing? Trying to make everyone hate me?

"Beg your pardon?" Dorothy put her hand to her chest.

"Is she off her trolley?" Maui cocked his head and looked at Heather. "Trying to get you turned into a toad on only your third day here?"

"No, I just... I was just asking. Listen, please, I'm new here. I'm just trying to learn about everyone... and someone killed my grandmother. I just want to find out who. That's all. Please don't take it personally." My voice was shaking.

Dorothy pursed her lips and I had a feeling she didn't believe me. It was one of those times where you feel absolutely alone even though you're surrounded by people.

"What are you doing?" I lowered my voice and spoke to Heather.

"If you want to find out what happened to Granny, then you need to start eliminating suspects. Might as well just get it all out there on the table." She shrugged. Did she seriously think she was helping? She lifted the chimichanga to her mouth.

"Dear, I can assure you, no one in this room hurt Granny," Tilly said calmly.

"Yeah, that's not what I was implying," Eve commented.

Heather cried out, startling everyone in the room. "Worms!" she spat. A collective involuntary retching came from nearly everyone in the room, myself included, as we saw bits of worms still hanging from Heather's open mouth.

"Oh, dear!" Minnie stood. "It's supposed to be chicken." She frowned.

"Gross!" Heather ran to the sink to rinse her mouth out, throwing the chimichanga in the trash on her way.

"See, Minnie? This always happens," Dorothy scolded.

"Serves her right," Maui said.

I caught Eve stifling laughter as she covered her mouth with her hand.

"Are you all right?" Tilly called over her shoulder to Heather.

Heather held her open mouth under the faucet and wiped her face with a paper towel before grabbing a cupcake from the table and holding it up. "Who made these?" she asked in a challenging tone.

"Mama did," Electra answered.

"Good." Heather peeled back the liner and bit into the cupcake. Guess she wasn't worried about being poisoned.

"You know, we don't know you either." Electra glared at me. She made a solid point.

"Yeah, you say you didn't know you were a witch, that you didn't know about Granny or any of us, but maybe you're lying. Maybe you're lying about a lot of things," Astra chimed in.

"Girls, stop," Peaches said, her voice still weak as she wiped the black streaks from under her eyes. "It ain't her fault someone used my cheesecake to poison Granny."

Now I really felt awful. Here she was, sticking up for me after I'd suspected her of murder and basically accused her in front of all the people she held dear. This was really not going well at all. I needed to change the subject.

"Cheris Sterling came by today," I remembered aloud.

"Mmm... watch out for that one." Minnie looked to Tilly for affirmation.

"Was she already in here trying to buy this place?" Tilly asked.

"Yes. There was also that woman claiming to be me," I said. "Honestly, those two are the ones that seem the most suspicious to me." I side-eyed Heather. "But I haven't found anyone who can say they saw either of them here the day Granny died."

"Well, until we know what really happened, we all need to be diligent. I suggest staying in pairs at the very least," Dorothy said.

"Boo," Eve mumbled, and Tilly nudged her with her foot.

"For everyone's safety, until we know what's really going on," Dorothy finished.

After I was outed as a possible defector by my one and only friend in town, there was more conversation as everyone made arrangements to accompany each other various places. I noticed Peaches and her daughters left right away though. She was still visibly upset and Astra and Electra stood on either side of her protectively, both shooting me angry looks as they headed for the door. I felt terrible.

I scanned the room again and spotted Eve standing on her own, munching on a second cupcake. She leaned against the counter and watched the group as if she was studying them. Then she turned to me abruptly, as if she'd felt me staring, and eyed me with intensity for a moment. It felt like her eyes were burrowing into my soul and my cheeks grew hot from the adrenaline jolt that fear gives you. She tossed the cupcake liner in the trash bin and made her way over to me. She came closer than I was comfortable with and lowered her voice.

"Be careful." Her icy gray eyes searched mine. "Someone may have very well killed Granny in order to bring you here.

You know that, right?" No, I actually hadn't thought of that. She paused.

"Until we know the truth, trust no one. Not even me. You got that?" she spoke with an urgent tone and grabbed my arm a little too hard.

I nodded. I didn't get the feeling that Eve was someone you disagreed with.

An hour ago, I had been thinking I was going to solve the mystery of who killed my grandmother and Trixie. Now, as fate would have it, not only did I need to solve those crimes, I needed to solve them quickly before I became the next victim.

CHAPTER 11

or the first time since I'd arrived in Blackwood Bay, I had spent the night alone, aside from Maui keeping me company. I had a feeling Granny was there—after all, she was stuck with me until I learned everything I needed to know about my magic—but she was hiding from me. She must've known there were some questions I had for her and I didn't know why she wouldn't want to answer them. Maui didn't know where Trixie had disappeared to either.

It would have been wonderful to get a full night's sleep since I was finally given some peace and quiet, but my thoughts kept me up all night. Witch hunters and dark witches and people who wanted Granny's building so bad they might have killed for it. It was disconcerting, and I admit I was scared. Maui stayed up most of the night, promising to let me know if he heard or saw anything, but I still couldn't manage more than a few hours. I'd made my way down to the bookstore a little before 9 a.m., when I knew Heather would be arriving to open up.

She was already flipping on the lights when I came through the stairwell door.

"Good morning!" she said brightly. I was still mad at her after the little stunt she had pulled the night before.

"Hey," I said, sipping coffee from a mug I'd brought down with me.

"You're mad, huh?" She furrowed her brow.

"Heather, you basically told everyone that I had accused them of murder. I just got here. Let them at least get to know me so they can dislike me for me." I said.

She laughed. "No one dislikes you. I wasn't trying to upset anyone. I just thought we needed to get everything out on the table. Everyone needs to be on the same page because we all want to find out what happened to Granny and Trixie."

I was contemplating what to say next when she said, "I just don't want what happened to my coven to happen here. It's important we all stick together." Yeah, except it felt like she was trying to pit them against me last night.

I nodded. I was still irritated with her, but Eve's words came to the forefront of my mind and I decided to let last night's events go for the time being.

"Anyway, I need to try to call my dad and Mitch Powders again," I said.

"I'll give you some privacy then. I have to unpack a few boxes of inventory anyway. Good luck." Heather smiled and headed to the back of the bookstore.

I pulled out my cell phone and tried Mitch Powders first. Straight to voicemail for the hundredth time.

I dialed my dad's number next and he finally answered on the second ring.

"Dru?"

"Dad! Finally! I tried calling you all day yesterday," I said.

"I know, I'm so sorry. I've been a little... tied up. But, honestly, I was also dreading talking to you." Gee, thanks, Dad.

"Honey, I've been feeling so guilty about everything and I just didn't even know what to say to you. Mostly because sorry just isn't good enough." He paused. "But also because I still think you made a mistake." Here we go.

"Dad—"

"It's not safe there, Dru," he said firmly. He was right, actually, but I didn't want him to worry any more than he already was.

"Dad, it's fine. I've met everyone in the coven and they're all looking out for me. I've even met the police chief and made friends with a sergeant. I'm safe."

"You have no idea whether you're safe or not. Besides, Granny and that girl, Trixie, were both murdered—"

"Wait, how did you know that?" I cut him off.

"Chief Carver is an old friend, Dru. He called me and filled me in on what's going on there."

I groaned. "Dad, I'm staying safe, okay?" How did this phone call that should've been him begging for forgiveness devolve into one of his lectures?

"I think maybe you should come back home. At least until they find out what's going on around there."

"Dad, I love you, but I am a grown woman, not a child. I am not running home to my daddy at the first sign of trouble here."

"Why? You had no problem doing that when you found out about Jason and Keely." He was right; I had run straight home, a blubbering mess, after I'd found out my ex-fiancé and my childhood best friend had been seeing each other behind my back. My dad had babied me and let me spend my days in pajamas binge-watching a women's movie channel network and eating junk food, right up until the call from my grandmother's lawyer came. Still, it felt like he was throwing it in my face now.

"Yes, I did. But that doesn't mean I have to do it again. Besides, everything is different now—" I saw a man approaching the bookstore through the front windows. He looked well-put-together, dressed in a two-piece business suit with his salt and pepper hair carefully styled, but he had a timid, confused look on his face. Almost like he was looking for someone but he wasn't sure who.

My dad continued, "The only thing different is that you *know* you're a witch. You're still the same person, Dru. And you're still my daughter. Someone is murdering people there and I'm worried about you."

"I know, Dad—" The man walked through the door then. And I mean walked *through* the door. He did not open it; he just strolled right on through and looked directly at me.

"Uh, I'm going to have to call you back, Dad."

"Dru, wait—"

"Love you. Bye." I slid my cell phone into the back pocket of my khaki shorts.

"Hello? Can I help you?" I said hesitantly.

He looked around the bookstore and then back at me. "Are you talking to me?"

"I don't see anyone else here, do you?"

"No, but no one can see me either it seems," he said.

"Yeah, I just learned yesterday that seeing ghosts isn't very common," I joked.

He looked at me straight-faced for a moment before he burst out laughing. "This is fantastic!" he said. "Ah, I knew if there was any place in town that I might be able to find help, this was it." He shook his head in disbelief.

"You need help?" I asked. Just what I needed: another ghost who needed my help.

His face turned serious. "Yes, very badly. Well, not me so much. It's my dog, Bear. You see, my body is in a very inconvenient spot, tucked away behind some driftwood and brush on the beach, and it hasn't been discovered yet. My dog has been home all alone for days now and she'll die if no one finds me soon. Please, you have to help."

"Yes, of course. Poor thing." I took one last swig from my coffee mug and hurried out from behind the counter.

"Heather, I have to go! Be back soon!" I called out.

"Is everything all right?" She peeked her head out from behind the tie-dye curtain.

"Yes, fine. I'll explain later!" I followed the ghost man out the door. I actually had to open it though, and we headed down the street toward the beach.

"Thank you so much for doing this. I've been going back and forth between checking on Bear and wandering around that stupid beach waiting for someone to find me. Being a ghost isn't as neat as people might think, you know. I mean, yes, you can walk through walls and teleport yourself whenever you want, but you're really helpless in a lot of ways too." I hadn't really thought about that before, and I felt a twinge of pity for both Granny and Trixie.

"I'm happy to help. I'm Dru, by the way. I don't think I caught your name."

"Oh, apologies. In my haste I don't think I gave it." He smiled. "The name's Mitch Powders."

123

CHAPTER 12

I stopped dead in my tracks.

"Mitch Powders?"

He nodded.

"Are you kidding me?"

He answered with a look of confusion.

"I'm Drusilla Rathmore Davis. Drusilla Rathmore's granddaughter."

He furrowed his brow. "Yes, I know Granny."

"I've been calling you for days! You need to tell me what is going on right now!"

"Ma'am, I don't think I understand. I told you... my dog needs help."

I searched his eyes. "Why are you looking at me like you don't know who I am?"

"I don't mean to be rude if we've met before. I seem to have experienced some memory loss post-death." *Great.*

I noticed a few people had stopped to stare at the crazy lady talking to herself in the middle of town and I lowered my voice as I started walking again. I filled him in on how he'd called me about a living trust that Granny never had made.

"I am a bit confused, and there is a lot I don't remember, but I don't think I'd do something like that. I don't know *why* I would do something like that either."

"Do you know Cheris Sterling?" I asked.

He rolled his eyes. "Everyone knows Cheris Sterling."

"She's been trying to buy Granny's building for years. Do you think she might've paid you off? Thought maybe her chances were better of getting me to sell?"

He shrugged. "I don't think I was an unethical man. And that would certainly be unethical."

I told him about Fake-Dru but he had no ideas about her either. We were getting nowhere. I needed to try something different.

"Okay, do you remember anything about how you died?"

He looked thoughtful for a moment before shaking his head. "I think... I think I was supposed to meet someone. Maybe. I remember hurrying down the beach and feeling like I was late. And I was in my suit, which is an odd thing to wear to the beach. But that's all I can remember."

"Were you planning on taking an unexpected vacation? That's what your receptionist said. She said you left a note."

Mitch thought for a moment. "I don't recall a vacation. I don't think I would've just left like that. That doesn't sound right." I couldn't be sure that he was telling the truth, but I decided to take him at his word for the time being.

We were approaching a pile of driftwood near a grassy embankment, stacked nearly five feet high, with jutted, sharp edges sticking out violently in various directions.

"I'm just behind there." He pointed and led me to a small

cave-like opening facing away from the beach. I peered inside and saw the soles of a man's oxfords.

"I'm not going to go in," I told him.

"I wouldn't," he agreed.

I pulled my cell phone from my back pocket and started to dial 911 when I was interrupted.

"Are you all right, miss?" A man was walking toward me and I wondered if he'd seen me talking to myself. He looked like he'd been out for a morning run on the beach. He pulled his earbuds from his ears and gave me a kind smile.

"Yeah, I'm fine. Except I think I stumbled on a body." I wasn't really sure how to explain and I looked to Mitch Powders, who gave me a shrug.

"A body?" The man's face fell and he rubbed the back of his neck with his hand. He came close and leaned to look inside the small opening that I was pointing at. He smelled like sweat and the salty breeze from the sea.

"Wow." He looked back up at me. "Have you called 911 yet?"

"I was just getting ready to," I answered.

"I can do it. Here, why don't you sit down?" He put his arm around me and led me to a pile of large boulders a handful of yards away.

"What's your name?" he asked, kneeling in front of me. I realized he must've thought I was in shock at finding a dead body on the beach.

"Dru," I said, and noticed Mitch smiling behind him.

"I'm Christian. Just stay here, okay? I'm going to call 911." He pulled a cell phone from the armband around his bicep and started walking back toward the spot where I'd found Mitch.

"Nice fella. A real gentleman." Mitch seemed amused.

"What's that supposed to mean?" I tried to whisper.

"He's taking awfully good care of you, don't you think?"

"He's a nice man helping a stranger who he thinks has just been traumatized."

"Whatever you say." Mitch shrugged but gave me a wink.

I scanned the beach hoping no one had seen me talking to myself again when I spotted him. The man in the navy shark hat. He stood about forty yards away and was staring right at me.

"Mitch, do you see that man over there in the dark hat and black jacket?"

Mitch turned and nodded.

"Do you know him? Does he live here?"

"I don't recognize him. We get a lot of tourists here though. Especially in the summer months. He kind of looks like a fisherman," Mitch said.

"I agree. The problem is I keep seeing him almost everywhere I go."

"Well, that *is* odd," Mitch said.

"They're on their way," Christian called out, his hand covering the mouthpiece. "They want me to stay on the line until they get here."

I nodded at him.

"I think he might be stalking me," I said to Mitch.

"Who? The handsome jogger?"

I rolled my eyes. "No, the man in the hat."

"You need to tell someone then. Tell the police when they get here, okay?" He knitted his brow.

"I did."

"Tell them again. You need to be careful. Someone killed me, I think."

"You aren't the only one," I mumbled.

"I have to go now. Thank you for helping me. And please,

make sure someone gets to Bear as soon as possible, okay?" Mitch pleaded.

"I will," I promised. And with that, he disappeared.

"You still doing okay?" I hadn't heard Christian come up beside me, and he planted himself on the boulder next to me.

"Yeah, I'm fine. Really," I said.

"Stuff like this never happens around here. I'm so sorry you had to find that body."

"I've had a crazy week so far," I said. "This might not even be the worst thing that's happened."

He looked confused. "Well, I hope you won't let it scare you off. Blackwood Bay is actually a wonderful place. How long are you visiting for?"

"Oh, I'm not visiting. I just moved here. I now own the bookstore on Hemlock."

"Ah, yes, Invoke," he said in a dramatic tone. "Very cool. Well, welcome."

"Thanks." I glanced over onto the beach and saw that the man in the navy shark hat was making his way toward us. I felt fear rise up in the form of a lump in my throat.

"What's wrong?" Christian asked and I guessed he must've seen something in my face.

"That man," I started.

"Dru?" It amazed me that I recognized that voice already. I turned to see Harper coming up the other side of the beach, running toward us, also dressed as if he'd been out for a morning run. Did every hot man in this town jog on the beach?

I waved as he approached, his brow creased with concern.

"Hey, who is this?" he motioned to Christian.

"Christian Fuller." Christian extended his hand to shake Harper's.

"Sergeant Harper," Harper gruffed. Did he always introduce himself as a cop?

"Are you here about the call I made?" Christian seemed unfazed.

"Yeah. I was taking a run, and Chief Carver called my cell." I heard police sirens approaching. I looked back to the beach, but the man in the shark hat had disappeared.

"What's going on? Are you all right?" Harper spoke to me in a much gentler tone than the one he'd used with Christian.

"Yeah, I'm fine. I just found a body."

He eyed me for a moment and started to say something when an officer approached and pulled him away.

"You sure you're all right? Something like this can be very traumatizing." Christian put his hand on the back of my arm.

"Dru!" Harper called. "I need to speak with you. Sir, Officer Dobson here will take your statement." Officer Dobson hurried over to Christian, a notepad in one hand and pen poised above it in the other. Harper motioned for me and led me up the embankment toward a handful of police cars, keeping his hand at my back.

"Are you mad or something?" I asked Harper.

He still had a scrunched-up brow. "No, why?" He asked.

"I don't know. You're being weird."

"I'm not being weird." He put his hands on his hips and the slight motion sent the scent of his aftershave wafting through the air. "So, why don't you start from the beginning?" He changed the subject.

"Okay, I was out here on the beach—"

"With that guy over there?" he motioned to Christian. Wait, wait, wait. Was he jealous?

"No, not with him. I was here by myself at first—"

"So you met him here? It's not very safe to just start talking to strange men on the beach with everything that's been going on around here." He did have a point, and I felt embarrassed that I had jumped to the assumption that he was jealous. Had I wanted him to be?

"No, I found the body and then he saw me and asked if I was okay—" I started again.

"Where did he come from?" Harper crossed his arms over his chest.

"Are you going to let me tell you what happened or are you going to keep interrupting?" I was getting annoyed.

Harper sighed and rolled his neck. "I'm sorry. You're right. Please continue."

"Anyway, I was down here walking along the beach and I came to check out that cool pile of driftwood over there—"

"Aren't you supposed to be working?" he asked.

"Sorry?"

"It's a weekday morning. You just leave work to go for walks on the beach?"

I groaned. "Seriously?"

He nodded and ran his tongue along the back of his teeth.

"Heather is at the store. I just needed to clear my head so I came for a walk. I saw the man's shoes in there and was getting ready to call 911 when Christian came along, so he called."

"Who is Christian?"

"Really? The guy I was with when you got here. The one you think is so dangerous," I quipped.

"I thought you didn't know him." Harper maintained a serious look on his face.

"I don't! He introduced himself to me the same way he did to you. You are being super weird right now. What is your deal?" I couldn't hide my annoyance any longer.

"No deal. It's my job to ask questions," he answered mildly.

A stretcher carrying a person-sized black bag was coming toward us. I needed to let Harper know about Mitch's dog but I also couldn't let on that I knew who the body belonged to since I had never met Mitch while he was alive.

"Do you know who that is?" I motioned to the stretcher.

"Don't look." Harper put an arm around me protectively and turned me away. "Yes."

"Who?"

"It's Mitch Powders."

"Granny's lawyer." I tried to sound surprised.

Harper nodded.

"I think he had a dog." I know, not very smooth.

"A dog?"

"Yes, I think he had a dog. I heard that somewhere. Can you have someone go to his house and check? I'm worried about the poor thing being there all alone."

"Of course," Harper said. "Bates! Can you have someone go over to Powders' house and see if his dog is there?" A uniformed officer nodded. "Give me a call if so. We'll have to find a way into the house since his mother is away. Speaking of, someone needs to find out how to contact Gloria Powders. I've been told she's gone off on a safari trip through Africa. Isn't due back for a few more weeks." Harper turned back to me. "Poor woman. What a terrible way to end a vacation."

"Thank you," I said and contemplated whether it would be wise to visit Gloria Powders when she returned just to let her know her son was okay.

"Have you found Tiffany yet?" I asked about the Fake-Dru.

"Unfortunately, no. It's possible she skipped town already, but we're still looking for her."

I nodded. "Thanks."

"I need you to be very cautious, okay? Don't go out on solo

walks along the beach, stay in after dark, make sure someone is with you if you decide to leave the bookstore, and don't eat anything you haven't prepared yourself," Harper said. I noticed a small line between his eyebrows and thought it must've been from knitting them together so much.

"I'm not going to live like a prisoner," I muttered.

"Dru, it's important. Someone killed Granny and Trixie, and now we've found Mitch Powders dead. Someone is obviously after something and I'm very concerned you could be a target as well. I need you to stay safe." He put his hands on the back of my arms but kept his touch light despite the urgency of his voice.

"I understand that. I do. But if it was someone close to Granny and Trixie, then I'm not really safe no matter what I do." It was the first time I'd said it out loud and the thought made my stomach flip.

He clenched his jaw. "Maybe you should go back home. Just until we get this figured out."

"I'm going back as soon as we're done here. I have to get back to work anyway, remember?" I attempted to tease him in order to lighten the mood.

"No, I mean *home* home," he said.

"Have you been talking to my father?" It wouldn't have surprised me if he'd said yes.

"Pardon?"

"You sound just like him. Look, I get that I'm most likely in danger here, but I'm not stupid. I'll worry about taking care of myself and you worry about solving these murders. How about that?"

I could tell he was exasperated but instead of arguing, he just said, "Okay, Dru." A look of defeat appeared in his eyes.

"Excuse me?" Christian approached.

"What?" Harper barked.

"I'm done speaking with Officer Dobson. Dru, if you'd like me to wait for you, I can walk you home."

"That won't be necessary," Harper said dismissively. "I can drive her."

"I don't mind," Christian challenged. "Dru, what would *you* like to do?"

"Sergeant?" A policewoman donning blue gloves called out near the pile of driftwood.

"Don't you have to stay, anyway, Officer?" Christian said. He was right; Harper couldn't really leave a crime scene, could he?

Harper hesitated, sizing Christian up. He took a moment to scan the beach like he was looking for something. After a few moments of tense silence, he finally said, "Okay. Dru, if you'd like him to walk you home, I can't stop you. Please let me know you got there safely."

He turned abruptly and headed toward his colleagues and I immediately felt a sense of guilt, though I wasn't entirely sure why. It was almost as if I'd disappointed him or hurt his feelings somehow. But he was a police officer and I was a crime scene witness. And that was all, right?

"Ready?" Christian gave me a big smile and I nodded.

∼

My walk back to the bookstore with Christian was filled with his attempts at making small talk and me doing a terrible job reciprocating. I had so many other thoughts racing through my mind. I should've been focused on Granny and Trixie and now Mitch, but my mind kept wandering back to Harper's strange behavior. Before I knew it, we'd reached the front of the store.

"Well, this is me," I said. "Thank you for walking me home. And for coming to my aid today."

"No problem." He smiled. "It was a pretty terrible way to meet. Hopefully next time it's under better conditions." I suddenly had a sinking feeling he was getting ready to ask me out.

"Yeah, well, I'll see you." I turned and hurried into the bookstore. I felt terrible, but it had to be done.

Christian was handsome, and sweet, but I had way too much on my plate to even think about trying to date anyone. Also, there was Harper. I barely knew him and yet, the mere thought of him made my heart leap and he occupied my thoughts more often than I was ready to admit.

CHAPTER 13

"Where have you been?" Heather was visibly perturbed as I walked through the front door, standing with her hip jutted out and arms over her chest.

"I'm sorry. I found a dead body," I said matter-of-factly.

"A dead body?" Her posture instantly changed and she widened her eyes. "Oh my gosh! Where?"

"The beach. It was Mitch Powders, the lawyer."

"Wow." Heather looked shocked.

"I know. Everything's a mess." I was feeling really overwhelmed with the reality of it all and walked around the counter to sit on the barstool.

"Is that why you ran out of here earlier? Did he, like, pay you a visit from the afterlife or something?" she asked.

I started to answer her honestly, but something stopped me. "No, I had something else to do." After the way she'd outed me the night before, I decided I needed to keep her at a distance for a while until she proved herself trustworthy.

She eyed me for a moment. "Don't stress, okay?"

Don't stress? How in the world was I supposed to not stress?

"Hey, I hate to do this to you, but I have a doctor's appointment so I really need to run. I'm already late." She started walking toward the back to retrieve her purse.

"Yeah, no problem," I muttered.

"I'll be back as soon as I can." She waved as she headed out the door.

"Are you okay?" I heard Trixie's voice from behind me.

"Trixie! Where have you been?" I was so relieved to see her. She was one of the only people I could really trust, and I was in desperate need of a friendly face.

"I'm sorry. Granny said we had to hide, but I missed you. She'll be mad if she knows I'm here," she whispered.

"Why do you have to hide?"

"I'm not supposed to tell." She twirled a blonde pigtail around her finger.

"I won't tell that you told me. Promise." It felt like negotiating with a child.

"She said that you were going to have lots of questions but we couldn't answer them yet. Something about your dad, I think."

"Granny!" I called out. "Is she in here? Can you see her if I can't?" I asked.

"Yeah, but she's not down here."

"She's upstairs?" I asked.

Trixie nodded. I stumbled trying to get off the barstool and knocked it over in my anger-fueled haste. I bent down and reached out my hand and it righted itself so fast I almost didn't realize what had happened. That's when I heard a voice behind me.

"Are you all right?" I turned to see a woman had come into the bookstore. I panicked. Had she seen that?

"Uh, yes, fine," I said, flustered, and smoothed the hair from my face.

"I didn't mean to sneak up on you," she said with a thick Irish accent. She looked exactly the way you'd expect an Irish woman to look. Natural red hair falling in perfect spirals around her face, porcelain skin, and freckles on her freckles.

"No worries," I said. "How can I help you?"

She leaned forward, her long red hair falling over her shoulders, covering the fluorescent green tie-dyed 'Cancun' T-shirt she was wearing. She studied me. "I haven't seen you in here before."

I didn't recognize her from the coven meeting the night before. Maybe she hadn't attended? Or maybe she wasn't a witch at all?

"I've only been here a few days. I'm the new owner."

"Of course. I was hoping I'd get to meet you before I left town." A smile formed on her lips. "My name is Brigid O'Malley." She held out her hand and gave me a firm handshake.

"Dru Davis," I introduced myself.

"Yes, I know." She winked. "I've known Drusilla for years and years."

"Are you..." I still hadn't quite worked out how to ask people if they were witches.

"Am I? You mean, can I pick up stools with my mind too?" She gave me a quick wink. "Yes, I can." I was both relieved and embarrassed. I needed to be much more careful with using my magic. Except I hadn't used it on purpose at all yet. How was I supposed to control it? More importantly, how had I seemingly controlled it my entire life up until a few days ago? Honestly, I was tempted to ask this stranger, because I was sick of everyone around me knowing things about me that I didn't.

"I don't recognize you. You weren't at our meeting last night, right?" I asked instead.

"Oh, no. I don't live in Blackwood Bay. I'm just passing through." She flicked her wrist. "I'm spending my summer making a trek up the West Coast stopping in at all of my favorite little coastal towns. Blackwood Bay has always been my favorite. For obvious reasons." She waved her hand around to indicate she was talking about the bookstore.

"Wow. That sounds incredible. I would love to do something like that one day."

She nodded. "What's stopping you? Don't wait your whole life for the things you want. Go out and get them." She chuckled and then a somberness fell over her. "I wasted too many years on dead-end jobs and dead-end men. Don't be like me. Live the life you want now. Tomorrow isn't a guarantee."

"That's fantastic advice." I smiled.

"My condolences about your grandmother, by the way. She was a great lady." Brigid smiled. "Is she here now?"

I shook my head. "She's hiding from me at the moment."

Laughter escaped her lips. "I'm sure she thinks she has a very good reason for doing so."

"I suppose you're right. She's difficult sometimes," I thought aloud.

"She is," Brigid agreed, "but only in the best possible way." I highly doubted that and wondered if she'd said it just in case Granny was listening.

"Anyway," Brigid said, "the reason I actually came in today—I'm getting ready to catch a ferry out of here and head on up north. About a week or so ago I came in and that poor young girl that worked here, Trixie," she paused waiting for me to nod in understanding, "she had set aside a book for me. I asked her to hang on to it until I was ready to leave. I've already paid in cash. I just need to pick it up."

"Oh! Yes, I remember," Trixie piped up. I'd almost forgotten she was there. "It's right there under the counter in a purple plastic bag. A copy of the receipt is taped to the front."

I pulled the bag out from a shelf under the counter and handed it to Brigid.

"Oh, wonderful!" she exclaimed. "I've been dying to read this but I knew if I had it with me, I'd spend the entire time I was here locked away in my hotel room curled up with this book. I wanted to save it for my ferry ride."

"I hope you enjoy it," I said.

"Oh, I will! Thank you. Good luck, lass. Oh, and remember, take as many new adventures as your bank account allows!" She laughed and gave a little wave as she made her way out of the bookstore.

Trixie giggled. "I remember her from last time she came in here. She's nice, but she's silly."

I leaned against the counter and faced Trixie. "Silly?"

Trixie nodded enthusiastically.

"I mean, she's a little eccentric maybe, but she seemed normal to me."

"Yeah, but she said she knew Heather but she didn't."

"What do you mean?" I asked.

"When she came in here last week, Heather was here too. She acted like she knew her but Heather said she didn't," Trixie explained.

I felt goosebumps rising up on my arm, but I wasn't sure why yet. "Trixie, start at the beginning. Tell me what they both said."

She rolled her eyes and put on a fake Irish accent. "Oh, Katie! I can't believe it's you! What are you doing here?"

Trixie turned to face where she had been standing before, pretending as if she was speaking to another person and used a high-pitched voice. "I'm not Katie."

"Sorry?" She jumped back to her original position. "I'm not Katie."

"Yes, yes you are. Katie, what happened to you? We were all so worried about you—"

"I'm not Katie!" Trixie yelled.

"Then Heather told me she had to leave and she left. That's what happened." Trixie turned to face me.

"Did you ask the lady about it after Heather left?"

Trixie shook her head. "No."

"Okay, thanks, Trixie." I grabbed my keys from my purse under the counter. "I'll be right back."

I burst through the front door of the bookstore and scanned the street for Brigid. I had to ask her about Heather. I had a feeling she wasn't a 'silly' lady at all and perhaps she knew something that I needed to know too. I locked the front door of the bookstore and started off toward Main Street. Brigid had said she was going to catch a ferry, and I was hoping to catch up with her before she boarded.

I rounded the corner and I saw him. Standing a few feet behind the back of the bookstore near the dumpster. There was no question now: he was following me. We locked eyes and this time he didn't turn away or run. I felt my heart slamming in my chest.

It was time, I decided, and I began walking toward the man in the navy shark hat.

CHAPTER 14

"*H*ey!" I had every intention of an intimidating, throaty shout, but instead it came out a shaky, high-pitched shriek.

He winced, not out of fear but due to my ear-piercing tone, no doubt. *Not a good start, Dru.*

"Why have you been following me?" He was quite tall and I couldn't exactly loom over him, so I kept my distance. A good five feet between us. Just out of his reach if he tried to grab me.

He stared at me for a moment and there was something strangely familiar about him, though I couldn't quite place it.

"Well?" I folded my arms across my chest.

"I was hoping you hadn't noticed," he finally said.

"Well, I did!" I sputtered. "What kind of an explanation is that anyway?"

"We need to go somewhere private to talk." He remained calm, shoving his hands into his pockets.

"You have got to be out of your mind to think I'm going somewhere private with the guy who's been stalking me."

"You have a valid point," he looked thoughtful for a

moment, "but I haven't been stalking you exactly. I've just been keeping an eye on you. Making sure you're safe."

"Why? Who are you?" I demanded.

"It's me, Dru." He took a step toward me and I instinctively put my hand up.

"Don't come any closer!" I shouted.

"I can prove it to you." He lowered his voice. "But not out here. We need to go inside at least."

"I'm not going anywhere with you until you tell me who you are and why you've been 'keeping an eye on me,'" I said, making air quotes with my hands.

"Dru. It's me. Dad," he said.

I laughed. "You're not my dad." Unbelievable.

"I am. And I can explain everything but we have to do it somewhere else, okay?" I watched his eyes scan the street behind me.

"You're crazy. I'm calling the police." I pulled my cell phone from my back pocket and started backing away, keeping my eyes on him.

"Wait!" He held out his hand. "You have a strange birth-mark right in the center of your torso. It's the same as the symbol on the doorknob to Granny's apartment."

How did he know about my birthmark? Or about what the doorknob looked like to Granny's upstairs apartment?

"I never told you this, but you weren't born with it, exactly. It's in the shape of the Witch's Knot. It's a symbol to protect against evil and evil spells. It appeared on your skin after your Granny covered you in a protection spell."

"This is madness. You've obviously been watching me long enough to know far more about me than you could've figured out in the last few days." I typed nine into my phone.

"No, please!" He took another step toward me and I automatically stepped back. "When you were a kid, I'd take you with me on stakeouts. The ones I knew were safe. We'd get Chinese food and a dozen donuts. You'd always make me open my own fortune cookie but then you'd snatch it from my hand and eat it. You liked maple bars the best. You'd read me chapters from whatever book I made you take along. The scary stories were our favorites." He stepped forward again and this time I stood frozen in place.

"Jason was your first love and your first heartbreak. After Timmy O'Brien, of course. Remember he asked you to be his girlfriend in second grade and then when you caught him holding hands with another little girl at recess you pushed him down in a mud puddle and socked him in the stomach." He laughed. "I was tailing a murder suspect that day and had to leave to come pick you up from school because they'd suspended you." He shook his head. I could feel a lump forming in my throat.

"How could you possibly know all that?" I managed barely above a whisper.

"I told you, Dru. It's me. It's Dad." I realized it then. The thing that had been familiar about him. It was the eyes. They weren't particularly distinct in color or shape, a chocolate brown, unlike my own. But they had a softness in them that I recognized.

I could feel myself beginning to shake. "But you don't look like my dad," I choked out.

"It's complicated. Which is why we need to go inside so we can talk privately."

I considered it, though my mind was jumbled with a plethora of competing thoughts. I did have my taser upstairs. And Granny and Trixie surely wouldn't let anything happen to me, if they could help it.

I nodded and headed back toward the bookstore, my mind racing but confident that he was close behind.

~

"*I*'m sick and tired of these cooking shows assuming everyone has fifty perfect little bowls to put the ingredients in. Grow up," Granny said the moment I walked through the apartment door. She was sitting on the sofa, a cooking show blaring on the TV.

I walked over and grabbed the remote from the coffee table and turned the power off. I turned back around to address the man in the shark hat, but was met with my father's face instead.

"Dad!" I exclaimed and all but jumped into his arms. I could feel the heat from my tears soaking his shirt.

"Hi, honey." He laughed and squeezed me in one of his bear hugs.

"Well, as I live and breathe," Granny said behind me. "Actually I'm not doing either at the moment. But I honestly thought I might never see that man again." She stood and walked toward us slowly, a wide grin on her face.

"Tell your father hello for me, would you? And give him a hug from me."

"Granny says hello," I wrapped him up in a second hug, "and that was from her."

"Hi, Granny," he said to the room, though she was standing right next to him. He lowered his head. "I'm sorry." His voice faltered. I looked at Granny but she said nothing, just nodding her head.

"Tell him I understand," she finally said. The raven cawed suddenly, breaking the silence that had filled the room. My dad turned and walked toward its cage.

"That was Granny's bird," I explained.

"Yes, I know," he said absently. "Hello, sweetheart," he said to the bird, unlocking the cage.

"I don't know if you should let it out, Dad. I don't want it flying around all over the place looking for a window to escape out of. I'd really like to talk to you too, so maybe you can play with the bird later. How did you do that anyway? Transform yourself into that other man?"

"She won't go anywhere," he said, completely ignoring my questions, more interested in the bird than me. The raven fluttered out of the cage and landed squarely on his shoulder. He laughed and I saw tears in his eyes.

"Dad—" I started.

"Shh," Granny interrupted me. "Let them have their moment."

"Granny, there's more pressing things here than my dad bonding with your weird bird," I whispered.

"You can't hear her yet, can you?" Granny turned to me and I saw tears welling in her eyes too.

"Who?" I asked.

"Your mother."

CHAPTER 15

"**W**hat do you mean? Where is she?" my eyes searched frantically around the room. How stupid of me not to realize that if I could see ghosts and my mother was dead, she certainly would come visit me.

"Really, Dru?" Granny threw her arms in the air in exasperation.

"What?"

My father laughed and I glanced up to see the raven softly pecking his ear. Granny motioned toward them with a flick of her wrist.

"The *bird* is a bird." Maui jumped up onto the window sill behind my father.

"Wait, you mean... but that doesn't make any sense. My mother died." I looked at Granny, but it was my dad who answered.

"That's one of the reasons I'm here, Dru." He walked toward me, the raven—or, my mother—still perched on his shoulder.

"Sit down. We need to talk." My head was reeling, and I let

my father lead me to the sofa. Maui jetted over, positioning himself in my lap. The warmth of his body provided some familiar comfort.

I felt my cell phone buzz in my pocket and I pulled it out: *Did you make it home all right? You never texted me.* It was Harper. I shot him a quick reply. *Yes, sorry. Something came up and I forgot.*

I turned my attention back to my dad. "Please tell me what's going on. There's so much I don't know and I'm tired of it. I want to know everything," I said.

He nodded. "Granny probably didn't tell you much out of respect for me. I'm sure she knew I was coming." He turned and spoke into the room. "Thank you."

"Dad, she's literally standing right next to you."

"Sorry, it's not like I can see her." He rolled his head from side to side and I heard his neck crack. A habit he'd always had.

"Your mother and I, we grew up together here in Blackwood Bay. We fell in love and got married and then you came along—"

"I already know all that. Skip to the bizarre stuff, please," I interrupted.

He chuckled. "Patience. As you know, your mother was much more than a regular woman. She was a witch. A powerful one, like your Granny was, and like you will be one day. And I —I was her Guardian."

"Guardian?" I asked.

He nodded. "Before I fell in love with her, before we ever even really knew each other, I was sworn to protect her with my life. To serve as her Guardian. As you now know, I failed miserably." The raven cawed, interrupting him.

"You stop that right now, Byron Samuel Davis!" Granny shouted. "You tell him I said stop it!"

"Granny said stop it," I parroted.

He nodded and gave me a sad grin. "I'm sure she did."

"What do you mean you were her Guardian? Your overprotective personality makes a lot more sense now, by the way. But why did she need one?"

"Certain family lines of witches have Guardians. It started centuries ago and it's a tradition we've kept. To ensure that the line stays... alive."

"Wait, does that mean I have a Guardian too?"

He nodded.

"Who? How come I've never met him? Or her?" I wasn't exactly sure how it worked.

"Him," my dad answered. "And it's better if you don't know who he is."

"But why?"

"Because... because the relationship can become too personal. He has a very important job to do. You're safer if you keep your emotional distance from each other." Thoughts of my ex-fiancé, Jason, invaded my mind without warning. Was he my Guardian? Was that why things had fallen apart between us?

"Don't think for a second it's that scumbag. It's not him." Granny must've read my mind.

"Are you saying that because of you and Mom?" I asked my father.

He nodded. "Yes. I let my guard down too much. We were happy, our life was perfect, and I thought we were safe. I was so wrapped up in it all that I forgot I had a job to do."

"Are Guardians witches too then?"

He laughed and shook his head.

"Okay, well, forgive me for asking such a ridiculous question. But you've been following me around disguised as an entirely different person for the last few days."

"I'm a shapeshifter."

"Shapeshifter?" *You have got to be kidding me.*

"Yes."

"Okay, you're going to need to expand on that."

"Along with families of witches, there are families of shapeshifters. Long ago, we started working together to keep each other safe."

"Safe from who?" I asked.

"From enemies."

"If you're a shapeshifter, does that mean I'm like, half-shapeshifter, half-witch?"

"No. You only get to be one or the other. If you'd been a boy you would've been a shapeshifter."

I wiped my eyes and dragged my hands down my face in frustration. I'd wanted answers, but all they did was leave me more confused.

"Tell me what happened to my mother." I looked at the raven and she cawed, cocking her head to one side. I noticed Granny pacing out of the corner of my eye.

"You were just a tiny baby then. We lived here, in the apartment above this one. Back then, there was nothing behind the bookstore except a wild field that led into the forest." He leaned forward and rested his elbows on his knees. "Your mother, she loved animals. They loved her too. She was the kind who was always rescuing strays and nursing them back to health. Healing injured animals—"

"She could heal animals?" I interrupted.

"Yes, your mother—she could do anything." His eyes welled again. "Anyway, one night we were asleep in bed. It was late, probably around two in the morning. I woke up and your mother was gone. At first, I thought she'd gotten up with you, but you were still sound asleep in your bassinet. It was summertime and we'd had the window open and I could hear an animal that sounded like it was in pain. The wailing was so loud. I knew right away where your mother had gone.

"I was angry with her at first. She shouldn't have wandered off by herself in the night like that. I ran to the window and saw her making her way through the field, her hands bouncing across the tops of wildflowers as she went. I called out to her but she couldn't hear me. I spotted the injured animal about twenty yards from her, a fox, near the base of an old oak tree. He spotted me too, and that's when it hit me. Something was very wrong.

"I yelled for Granny and handed you to her as I ran from the apartment. I took the fire escape because it was quicker. I kept calling for her but she couldn't hear me over the wailing fox. I thought if I shapeshifted, I could catch her in time." He sniffed, the tears free flowing from his eyes now. My own vision blurred as hot tears spilled onto my cheeks.

"I wasn't fast enough, Dru." He shook his head.

"She was right there, right in front of the fox, and I knew I wouldn't make it in time. So I changed back into a man and called for her one last time. She heard me that time and she turned. It's the biggest regret of my life. I'd distracted her. The fox shifted into a man then and he killed her. Staring at me the entire time."

My dad stopped and wiped his eyes. "Then I heard a clap of thunder, and the biggest lightning bolt imaginable ripped through the sky. It hit him and he completely disappeared into thin air. I turned to see Granny watching from the window, holding you in her arms. The worst scream I'd ever heard came from her and I could see red glowing in her eyes."

"He disappeared?"

"Yes, he was thrown over five hundred feet away. Cops found him the next day."

"He's lucky I had a baby in my arms. He would've got it a lot worse if I hadn't." Granny was visibly shaking.

"So he was a shapeshifter too? But I thought you guys were Guardians? Why would he kill my mother?"

"We aren't all Guardians. Most of us are, but there's a few of us that are witch hunters."

"Witch hunters. I heard a little bit about those at the coven meeting last night."

"Certain shapeshifters, just like certain humans, have met dark witches or heard stories about them and it makes them afraid. So afraid that they dedicate their lives to hunting witches. Assuming all of you either are bad or will turn bad eventually. It's why Guardians came to exist in the first place. Whoever he was, he knew your mother was important. That's why he went after her. And it's why we had to leave."

"To keep me safe," I repeated the words I'd heard so many times.

He nodded, "If he came for her, then I knew someone would come for you. We just couldn't take the chance. So Granny worked some of her magic on you, and we left."

"What magic, Granny?" I asked.

"A protection spell, of course. And another."

"Another?" I prodded.

"Go ahead, Granny. We need to tell her the truth." My dad leaned back and petted the raven—er, my mother—with a single finger.

"It was an identity spell. Basically, you were bound from doing magic so you wouldn't learn who you truly were. Your power is strong though, I'm sure you had moments where the spell didn't hold it back completely. But it was the best I could do."

"So that's why I never knew I was a witch."

Granny nodded. "When I died, you were free from the spell. That was a precaution I had put into place. But it had been dormant for so long, I don't think it really awoke in you until you came here."

"That makes so much sense." I glanced back at my father. "Thank you for protecting me. I understand now why you did it." I scratched the top of Maui's head. "But what about my mother? She obviously didn't die if she's a raven now."

"No, not exactly. Her body did. But not her soul. Your mother, she had the ability to body-jump. Which is much different than shapeshifting. When she sensed she was going to die, she simply left her body and jumped into the nearest one. Which just so happened to be a raven, perched on the limb of an oak tree. So, she didn't truly die, but she no longer had her body. Of course, none of us knew that until months after you and I had gone."

"Nope. Just had some pesky bird that kept coming around and driving me batty. Couldn't figure out why it kept coming back after I'd shooed it away so many times," Granny said.

"Ma, tell her I had a difficult time learning to talk to humans in animal form. That's why none of you knew before Byron and Dru left. Tell her I'm so sorry. Tell her I wanted to go with them but wasn't able to tell anyone who I really was. Tell her, Ma. And tell her I thought about her every day. Tell her I love her," a soft, feminine voice filled the room. I knew I had only heard her voice as an infant, but somehow, I recognized it.

"Mom?" The word felt funny coming from my mouth, having never called anyone that before, and I stuttered through it.

Granny's head snapped in my direction. "Did you hear her?"

I nodded. "I think I did."

"What's going on?" My dad's face was knit with worry.

"Are you able to hear me now, sweetheart?" The woman's voice came again.

"I think... I think I can hear her speaking," I choked out.

She cawed. "You can! You can hear me!"

A nervous laugh escaped from somewhere deep inside me as I noted the huge grins on both my dad and Granny's faces.

"Oh, Dru! Oh, I have so much to tell you! And I have so many questions for you!" she said in a singsong voice.

A rapid banging came against the apartment door, and all of us jumped. Maui hissed and bolted from my lap.

Had my father not been there with me, I would've been hesitant to open it, but he'd always kept me safe. And it was still light out. Bad things only happened at night, didn't they?

I was shocked to see Dorothy standing there.

"Dorothy, hi."

"Dru, hello, dear. Listen, can you come downstairs please? It's urgent," she said. I realized she hadn't even noticed my dad.

"What is it?" I let my hand fall away from the doorknob.

"Heather has called an emergency meeting. Please, just come." She motioned for me to follow her and hurried back down the steps.

Heather had called an emergency meeting, huh? Well, good, because if I was going to confront Heather or Katie or whoever she was, I wanted witnesses. And who better than our entire coven?

CHAPTER 16

J hurried down the creaky wooden staircase, reciting in my mind exactly what I would say once I entered the bookstore. I had cleverly decided that I would call Heather 'Katie' to see what kind of reaction she would give me.

But when I rounded the corner, the sound of voices getting louder, I found a protective circle had formed around her. Minnie had her arm around her and Tilly was handing her tissues and speaking in a soothing voice. Heather's face was red and swollen and her eyes were bloodshot. I watched her shoulders heave as a hand over her mouth covered her sobs.

"What's going on?" I raised my voice so I could be heard over the commotion.

"Oh, Dru. Come on, darlin'." Peaches held her hand out to me and led me closer to the group. I guessed she'd forgiven me for what had happened the night before, which made me feel even worse than I already did. I gave her hand a little squeeze and she turned and gave me a quick wink.

"Everyone, quiet please. Quiet!" Dorothy commanded. The

voices died down but looks of uneasiness remained. "We have a very urgent matter to discuss," she said.

"Dru, where were you? You can't just close the bookstore in the middle of the day," Electra said, a wad of pink gum visible in her mouth. Well, it seemed she hadn't forgiven me even if her mother had.

"I'm sorry. I had a very urgent matter to deal with myself." My voice faltered.

Electra rolled her eyes and blew a pink bubble.

"It doesn't matter." Dorothy waved her hand dismissively. "Heather, are you able to do this, dear, or should I explain?"

Heather wiped her eyes with a tissue and sniffled. She stood and glanced around the room, her eyes lingering on me a few seconds longer than anyone else. "I think I can manage," she said.

"What's going on?" Minnie asked, confusion on her face. "Why are you crying?"

Dorothy shushed her. "She'll tell us if you'd be quiet."

"As you all know, my coven was taken out by a witch hunter." Heather paused while everyone nodded. "But there's something else I didn't tell you. I was just afraid that if I told you, you might not let me stay." She lowered her eyes.

Astra put an encouraging arm around her.

"The witch hunter that did it. It... he wasn't a man. He was a shapeshifter." Audible gasps filled the room.

"But we haven't heard of a shapeshifter witch hunter since... since..." Dorothy said, and everyone looked at me.

"Since my mother?" I said for them. "I know all about it now."

"Yes, since Aurora." Dorothy looked down at her hands.

"Could it have been the same one who killed her?" Heather's eyes widened.

"No, Granny took care of him," Peaches answered.

"You should've told us." Dorothy had an edge to her voice and she started pacing.

"I know. I'm sorry. I was so scared and I was afraid you wouldn't let me stay in case... in case he followed me here." Heather's voice cracked. "I knew this was the safest place I could be. I didn't want you all to make me leave." She started crying again.

"Oh, hush now. We wouldn't have made you leave." Peaches put her hand on Heather's shoulder and smoothed her hair.

"We might've," Dorothy quipped.

"Dorothy!" Minnie scolded.

"It's true." She shrugged. "What makes you think he would've followed you here anyway? I don't mean to be rude, but you aren't exactly from a powerful line, are you? You're just a dime-a-dozen witch. What would motivate him?" Dorothy raised a solid point, albeit harsh, and Heather narrowed her eyes.

"How would he have even known about you anyway? You said you saw him in the window. Did he see you?" she continued.

"I don't think so. But he easily could've figured out that there was one coven member not in attendance. As for why he would follow me, I am a witness, after all." Heather glared at Dorothy.

"I'm sorry, but why does any of this matter? It's been what? Two years. Why would he wait so long? Why are you telling us this now?" I broke the silence, surprising myself.

"Because Granny and Trixie are dead. I'm afraid he's come here and..." Heather buried her face in her hands.

"And?" Dorothy said.

"There's more. Right before Trixie died, a woman came into the bookstore. She said she recognized me and she called me by my real name, Katie."

"Your real name isn't Heather?" Electra asked, wide-eyed.

She shook her head. "I changed it. Fresh start and all. Anyway, there's no one left alive who knows me by that name. I was thinking it could've been him. He wanted to let me know he found me by playing some sick game. Coming in here, shifted into that woman and calling me by my real name."

"That woman was in here today," I spoke up. "She didn't mention you. Just came in to pick up the book she bought. But Trixie told me about the encounter you two had."

"I know. I saw her walking down the street. That's why I left earlier. I didn't really have a doctor's appointment. I'm sorry I lied to you. I was just so scared. I left and ran straight to Tilly's house so we could call for an emergency meeting. I can't believe this is happening. I can't believe he's here." Heather's eyes grew wide and a panic-stricken look crossed her face.

"Look at the receipt," Eve piped up. She'd been so quiet I hadn't noticed her.

"Sorry?" I said.

"The receipt. What name does it have on it?"

"She paid in cash," I said.

Heather plopped down on the sofa and ran her hand through her hair. "I'm so sorry. I am so, so sorry. I've brought this monster here. And now he's killed Granny and Trixie. It's all my fault!" She started sobbing uncontrollably.

"Thanks for that," Eve deadpanned.

An eruption of supportive voices began all at once. I noticed Dorothy was not participating; instead, she studied Heather with narrowed eyes.

Eve stared at the ground, fidgeting with the silver cuff on

her bicep. "What if this witch hunter doesn't have anything to do with their deaths though?" Eve said.

"How do you mean?" Dorothy asked.

"Well, maybe it's just coincidence. Maybe they were killed for some other reason and he just happened to show up around the same time. Maybe he didn't even know Heather was here. Or that a coven was here, for that matter," Eve supplied. She had moved on to twisting a large turquoise ring around her index finger.

"That's a possibility." Dorothy looked thoughtful.

"So, if this witch hunter is a shapeshifter too, then can he become anyone? Are there rules to this or what?" I asked.

"He can, yes," Dorothy said.

"In other words, he could be anyone. An old man walking down the street. He could shift into your neighbor, your friend. He could shift into you, or he could shift into me." Eve's icy gray eyes met mine and I felt a shiver run down my spine.

CHAPTER 17

"*N*o wonder you never remarried. You were roaring like a lawn mower all night." Granny stood behind my father, watching him stir sugar into his coffee. He had refused to leave for the night after I'd told him about the potential witch hunting shapeshifter in town. Instead, we'd stayed up almost until dawn, recounting stories from my childhood for my mother. It was the first time in my life I'd felt whole. Like the piece that had been missing was finally found.

"He can't hear you, Ma," my mother said, exasperated.

"Does he know you used to put a soundproofing spell around him every night so we could all get some sleep?" Granny asked.

"Would've been nice to have known that was an option for me growing up," I said.

"What's that?" my dad looked up at me expectantly.

"Nothing." I waved my hand. "When are you going back home?" I asked.

He pretended to look hurt. "You don't like having your old dad around?"

"I do. I was just curious."

"I really can't stay. I desperately want to, but I've already let everything get so far behind at work. I don't have anyone as reliable as you to fill in for me since you're gone." I ignored his attempt at a guilt trip.

"Hey, I was wondering... I know you're my dad and worrying about me is like in your blood, but if I have a Guardian, why did you come here to watch out for me?"

He let out a deep exhale before he spoke. "Well, when you were a kid you didn't need one yet, since you had me. In fact, you didn't *really* need him until you skipped town on your old man and came here." He paused for effect. "It's just hard for me to entrust you to someone else now. Not that I don't trust him, but it's hard to leave you in someone else's hands. You're my daughter."

"I know, Dad. But I can take care of myself too, you know. I don't need a man looking out for me all the time." I rolled my eyes.

"It's not about a *man* looking out for you. Under normal circumstances, if you were a regular human woman, I would agree completely. You're smart, stubborn, and strong. But we're dealing with things you don't fully understand yet. Magic and all that. Besides, your mother was the bravest, toughest woman I'd ever met but when the time came it didn't matter. One of her biggest strengths also became her weakness, and someone preyed on her knowing that. That's what a Guardian is for. Sometimes it's not to protect you from the world, but to protect you from yourself."

I nodded, trying to wrap my mind around all he'd just said.

"This is all great, really," Granny said, "but we have some big fish to fry. A killer to catch! You need to get to it."

"Ah, there it is," Maui said. "I was waiting for you to make this about you."

Granny shrugged. "I'm just practical."

"What are your plans today, Dru?" my mother asked, ignoring them both.

"My plans today," I said, looping my dad into the conversation, "are to snuff out the fake me. I still think she has something to do with all of this. And I'm going to visit Cheris Sterling."

My dad barked out a laugh. "Cheris Sterling. I haven't heard that name in ages. Is she still walking around like she's got something stuck up her butt?" he asked.

"Yes. She's kind of odd. She seems... nice, but also like she's completely faking it sometimes. I can't quite get a good read on her," I thought aloud.

"She's not nice. Trust me." My dad sipped his coffee.

"If you don't want me tagging along, then I should probably head to the airport and catch the next flight back home." He looked at me expectantly.

"Dad, I'm fine. Really. Please stop worrying about me so much."

He laughed. "I am always going to worry about you," he paused as if the next words pained him to say, "but I've been shadowing your Guardian these last four days just as much as I've been shadowing you. He's doing a fine job. You're in very good hands. I'm only a phone call away too. Besides," he chugged the last of his coffee, "you're forgetting that you're a witch. If there's a killer out there, a witch hunter, whatever, you have the ability to stop him. To keep yourself safe. You just have to stay vigilant." He stood and kissed the top of my forehead, "And don't eat anything someone else prepared for you."

"Was that a dig?" Granny asked. "Ask him if he was making a dig at me."

"It wasn't a dig, Ma," my mother said.

"It's kind of ironic that such a powerful witch was taken down by a simple piece of dessert," Maui mused. "Such irony."

Granny cursed him as I headed for the door.

"I'm coming with you," she said.

"Oh, me too!" Trixie jumped and clapped her hands in excitement.

I spun around. "What? No, you are *not* coming with me."

"I know?" My dad gave me a puzzled look.

"I wasn't talking to you." I waved him off.

"Yes, I am, and you can't stop me." Granny folded her arms over her chest.

I groaned. "Can't you two go haunt someone else for a while?"

Granny remained stoic and Trixie faked a pout.

"Just… just stay out of the way," I said, defeated.

"Fat chance of that happening." My dad laughed as I gave him a quick hug goodbye.

"Call you soon," I promised.

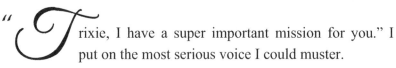

"Trixie, I have a super important mission for you." I put on the most serious voice I could muster.

"Ohh, what is it?" she whispered.

"Mitch Powders had a dog. I asked that police officer, Harper—"

"The cute one?" she interrupted.

"Yes, him. I asked him to make sure someone got the dog

from Mitch's house. I need you to find that dog and make sure he's okay. His name is Bear. Can you do that?"

She nodded, her pigtails bobbing on either side of her head.

"This is very important, Trixie," I said.

"Oh, I can do it! Don't worry, Dru!" Trixie exclaimed before disappearing into thin air.

"Don't think you're gonna get rid of *me* that easily." Granny jabbed her finger at her chest.

"Oh, I don't." I groaned and threw open the front door to the bookstore. "Tracking down Cheris Sterling first, but where do I find her? Does she have an office or something?" I asked Granny.

"I think she just hops around to her various inns, but I'm not really sure."

"Well, we'll start there and see if we can track her down. The closest one is right by the hardware store on Main Street, isn't it? Is the hardware store open yet?" I saw a few people heading toward me on the street and lowered my voice.

"Opens at seven. Why?"

"I want to buy a bell for the bookstore. Why don't you have a bell for that door anyway?" I asked.

Granny shrugged. "Never needed one."

"It's this way, right?" I knew I'd passed it at some point and I motioned down Main Street toward the Port.

"That's the way," Granny said.

"Okay. I can't keep talking to you though. Someone is going to see and call the cops on the crazy lady wandering around the streets."

Granny started to say something but I was distracted by my cell phone buzzing. It was a text from Heather.

Hey Dru. Don't think I can come in today. Yesterday was very draining for me emotionally and to be honest, I'm just

MISTY BANE

really scared to leave my house right now. I'm going to ask someone to come over and sit with me. I'm really sorry.

"What is it?" Granny asked.

"Heather. She's not coming into work today."

"And you plan to be out running around town. You can't keep a business open if it's never actually open, Dru."

"Yes, Granny, I realize that. But do you want me to find your killer or not?" I said.

"I do." She pursed her lips.

"Good. Once things calm down, I'll do a better job of running the bookstore. But I can't do everything at once," I said.

I understand. Let me know if you need anything.

I texted Heather and slid my cell phone back into my pocket.

"Almost there," Granny said.

I looked up and saw a sleek white sports car parked on the street near the entrance of the hardware store. I wouldn't have thought much of it, except rapid movement coming from inside caught my attention. I narrowed my eyes, peering into the car and I could just make out a woman.

She had lowered herself down in the passenger seat, a black baseball cap on her head and large dark sunglasses covering most of her face. But the white hair was hard to hide. She had her face turned a complete ninety degrees, and I had no doubt that she'd seen me and was trying to keep me from recognizing her.

"Granny?" I whispered. "That's her, isn't it?"

"That is! That's that little impostor!" she shouted.

"What do I do?" I froze. I wasn't sure if confronting her was the best course of action or if I should just call Harper. As I contemplated my next move, the door for the coffee shop next to the hardware store flew open, slamming me right in the face.

I cried out, covering my face as if that would stop the unbearable pain burning my nose. It felt like I'd been hit with a baseball bat.

"Oh! Oh, no! I'm so sorry!" I heard a man's voice and opened my eyes, cursing. I could feel the tears streaming down my face and through blurred vision I could just make out Christian's face.

"Christian?" My voice was shaky.

"Oh, Dru. I am so sorry! Here." He shuffled around for a moment, trying to figure out what to do with the two coffee cups in his hands before setting them on the ground, and shoved a handful of napkins at me. I held them to my bloody nose, willing the pain to subside.

"Are you okay? Is it broken?" he asked.

I shook my head. "No, I don't think so." I mumbled through the wad of napkins against my face. It still stung like crazy, but I didn't think it was broken.

"Stupid idiot." Granny sneered. "Shrink his head." That prompted a slight laugh out of me and Christian gave me a puzzled look.

"I'm fine, really," I said. Other than feeling embarrassed as I stood there with blood pouring down my face.

"Let me, um—can I take you home or something?" His voice had a nervous edge to it.

"No, we're good. It was an accident. I have errands to get to anyway."

"Okay." Concern clouded his face. "Listen, this is probably terrible timing, but I was planning on coming by the bookstore." He paused, "I'd really like—"

A car horn interrupted him and we both looked at the white sports car. A look of sheer panic was on Tiffany's face, and I guessed she'd accidentally touched the horn. She shrank down into the seat until only the top of her head was visible. Christian raised one hand in the air as if to say, 'what?'

"I'm sorry." He turned back to me, an annoyed look on his face. "My cousin has no manners whatsoever."

"Wait. Your cousin?" I asked.

He nodded. "Yeah, my cousin, Tiffany. First, she wanted me to drive down here and get her coffee—she loves this place," he motioned to the coffee shop, "but I told her I wasn't her errand boy and she'd have to come. Then when we get down here, she refuses to get out of the car. And now she's being incredibly rude while I try to have a conversation." He huffed.

"Tiffany is your cousin?!" I was incredulous.

"Yeah, do you know her or something?" Christian asked, but I was already blowing past him, a woman propelled forward by the need for answers. I stormed over to the car and banged my fist against the driver's side window.

"Whoa." I heard Christian come up next to me.

"Open the window!" I demanded but Tiffany had turned away. "You can't ignore me!" I shouted, but she was certainly trying.

"Get her, Dru! Knock her block off!" Granny cheered me on.

"Open this door! I need to talk to her!" I turned to Christian and lowered the napkins away from my face, certain that the blood had stopped. I knew I must've looked like something from a horror movie with blood all over the lower half of my face and neck, but I didn't care. He stared at me wide-eyed, but he obliged.

"Tiffany!" I said firmly.

She waited a moment before I saw her take a deep breath as she turned to face me.

"We need to talk." I lowered my voice to a reasonable level

but tried to maintain an intimidating edge. I have no idea if it worked.

"I don't have anything to say." She shook her head, staring at her lap.

"That's not an option," I replied.

"Can someone tell me what's going on?" Christian asked. I waited for Tiffany to respond, but she simply turned and looked out the window again.

"Your cousin here came into the bookstore a few days ago claiming to be me." I eyed him for a moment, the possibility that he could be a part of this finally dawning on me.

"What?" Christian made a face and leaned into the car to address Tiffany. "What's she talking about? What did you do?"

"Christian, my grandmother was murdered along with another girl in this town. And the guy we found dead on the beach? That was her lawyer. Your cousin shows up claiming to be me and I'm assuming it's so she can claim my inheritance. Although I'm not sure how she would even know about it or why she would want it, really."

"Hey!" Granny was obviously offended.

"Something seriously fishy is going on around here, and the cops are looking for her."

Tiffany's head spun toward me, her ponytail slapping the window. "The cops are looking for *me*?"

"Yeah, they are." I felt a sense of satisfaction watching her squirm.

"But I didn't even do anything illegal."

"We'll see about that, won't we?" I raised my eyebrows.

Christian cursed. "Dang it, Tiffany. What were you thinking? What is going on?"

"They want to question her in regards to the ongoing murder investigations, I'm guessing. Along with why she would be trying to pose as me." I folded my arms across my chest. The blip of a police siren came from behind and I turned to see Harper pulling his cruiser over to the curb.

"Impeccable timing," I said as he climbed out of his car.

"Wait, I'm sure there's a reasonable explanation for this." Christian held his hands up defensively.

"And what would that be?" I asked.

"What's going on?" Harper approached, his brow knitted together in its usual fashion, "What happened to your face? Are you hurt?"

I waved my hand. "I'm fine. Just a bloody nose. Listen, Tiffany Goldwait is in this car," I said triumphantly, and Harper bent to peer inside.

"Christian," Tiffany whimpered.

"Nice to see you again, Officer," Christian began. "Listen—"

"Save it." Harper held up his hand and walked around to the passenger side of the vehicle.

Christian turned to me, wide-eyed. "She said she didn't do anything. I'm sure there's some sort of misunderstanding. Look, my cousin is a spoiled brat—"

"Am not!" Tiffany cut in, stepping out from the car as Harper held the door open.

"But she's not a murderer," Christian finished.

"Tiffany, you're wanted for questioning in the murders of Drusilla Davis, Beatrix La Monte, and Mitch Powders. I'd also really like to know why you created a fake identity and claimed to be Dru Davis," Harper said gruffly.

"Oh, my god!" Tiffany wailed. "I didn't kill anybody! I would never! This has all gotten way out of hand."

"Calm down with the theatrics." Harper chuckled. "It's just questioning. You're not being arrested."

"What are you going to do now?" Christian asked.

"Just take her into the station and ask her some questions is all."

"Does she need a lawyer?"

Harper shrugged. "It's up to her."

"No! Listen!" Tiffany shrugged Harper's hand off of her arm. "None of this was my idea!"

"Whose idea was it then?" Harper asked, looking at Christian.

He held his hands up. "Look, man, this is the first I've heard about any of this."

"Not Mr. Goody Two Shoes." Tiffany rolled her eyes.

Harper put his hand gently on the small of her back and led her to his cruiser. I could hear her break out into sobs as she went.

"Stay in town. We'll be in touch," Harper called back over his shoulder, and I wasn't sure if he was talking to me or Christian.

"This is a mess. I can't believe this." Christian ran his hands through his hair and stared at the ground. I felt a surge of sympathy for him in that moment, and I realized that he was probably telling the truth about having no idea what his cousin had been up to.

His eyes met mine then. "I really don't think she hurt anyone." His voice was soft. "There's just no way. Tiffany is spoiled and self-absorbed and she's certainly materialistic, but she's not evil. There's just no way she would... *kill* anyone."

I wasn't sure how to respond, so instead I awkwardly twisted bloody napkins in my hands.

"I'm sorry about your grandmother, by the way," he said unexpectedly.

"Thanks." I offered him a smile and felt the dried blood crack on my face. Gross. I'd completely forgotten about it.

Christian sighed. "I guess I need to call my aunt."

"Tiffany's mother?" I asked.

He shook his head. "No, my other aunt. She's the sister of both my mom and Tiffany's mother. She lives here. It's why I'm visiting in the first place. I come for a month every summer." He pulled a cell phone from his pocket.

"Okay, well, I'll let you have some privacy. Sorry for ruining your morning." I shrugged, unsure of why *I* was apologizing.

He waved his hand. "You did no such thing. This isn't your fault." I was a little taken aback that he was being so kind despite the fact that I'd just had his cousin dragged off to the police station.

I nodded and started to walk away, hearing the first snippet of his phone call.

"Hey, Aunt Cheris. I need you to call me back right away…"

CHAPTER 18

I froze momentarily, but Granny prodded me along.

"Keep walking," she said. "We'll head her off at the police station. No doubt she'll show up there and try to smooth things over for her niece. You can hide in the bushes and we'll wait for her to show."

"I'm not hiding in the bushes. That's weird," I said, my head still reeling from just learning that Cheris was both Tiffany and Christian's aunt.

"Wait." I stopped. "I have blood all over my face. I need to get cleaned up first."

"We don't have time for you to go home. We might miss her."

"I know that. Is there like some kind of magic I can do?" I asked.

"Yes," Granny's eyes darted around, "but not here. Follow me." She turned and started heading back in the direction we'd just come from, and I noticed Christian's car was already gone.

"There's a public bathroom just down this way." Granny led

me to a bright blue building and I followed her inside the door marked WOMEN.

She scurried around, checking that all of the stalls were empty before giving me her attention. The bathroom was utterly disgusting with its streaked mirrors and the mud and sand-covered floor. I wasn't sure if my nose was burning from losing its fight with a door or from the wretched smell that filled the old concrete building.

"All right. We need to hurry. Close your eyes and concentrate," Granny instructed and I did as I was told.

"Now I want you to envision what you want," she said softly.

Envision what I want. Okay... well, no blood stains on my face and shirt would be a great start. I tried to picture myself when I'd left that morning, stain-free. Concentrate.

Ugh, it would be a lot easier if the smell of this bathroom wasn't ravaging my senses. It was starting to make me nauseous and I fought the urge to retch. *I mean, how hard is it to mop the floors, spray a little Windex on the mirrors, and could they please get some air fresheners in here? It's gross,* I thought. If it wasn't so nasty, I could concentrate. The scent of lemon and fresh lavender suddenly filled the room.

I opened one eye and saw Granny frowning, arms folded across her chest.

"Really, Dru?" she said. I opened the other eye and looked around. The bathroom had gone from a complete pigsty to a sparkling delight. The steel was shining, the mirrors were bright and clear, and the room smelled lovely.

"Did I—"

"Yes," she cut me off.

I clasped my hands together in excitement.

"Why are you happy about this? This is not what you were supposed to do."

"Because! Because that's the first time I've done something on purpose!"

"Yeah, except it wasn't on purpose. You were trying to do something entirely different," Granny pointed out. "Look, we don't have time for this. Grab some paper towels and wash your face," she said.

I yanked a handful of paper towels from the dispenser and set to work scrubbing the lower half of my face and neck.

"Hurry. We don't want to miss her. She could be showing up at the police station any minute."

"I'm trying!" I was exasperated, and I couldn't tell if my skin was stained or pink from rubbing it raw with rough paper towels.

The bathroom door flew open behind me and I jumped.

"Sorry to startle you." I heard a familiar Irish accent and spun around.

"Oh, hello again." It was Brigid, the traveling Irish witch from the bookstore the day before.

"Brigid. Hi," I said. A wave of fear hit me abruptly. What if this really was a witch hunter and not a sweet, old witch?

A look of worry was on her face. "Are you all right?"

"Oh, yes, fine. Just had a little accident, but I'm okay."

"My, I think this is the cleanest public bathroom I've ever seen!" she commented as she looked around. "And it smells divine, doesn't it?"

I couldn't help but smile, a sense of pride welling up in me.

Granny snorted. "Maybe you can start a cleaning service when the bookstore goes belly up."

"Yes, it's very nice," I said, watching Brigid as she stood in front of the mirror and finger-combed her hair. "I thought you were catching a ferry yesterday?"

"Oh," she grinned, "well, I was supposed to. But I met a very nice fellow after I left your bookstore yesterday. I stopped in for a quick lunch at that little café down by the beach and I saw this handsome chap sitting all alone. He kept making eyes at me, so I finally invited him to join me. He was wearing one of those captain's hats. Quite dim-witted, actually, but he was handsome."

She pulled a tube of lipstick from her purse and leaned into the mirror. "Anyway, we spent the afternoon on his yacht." Her eyes met mine in the mirror and she gave a half smile. "Spent the evening there too." She giggled. "So, I'm catching the ferry today instead."

"Scandalous," Granny quipped.

"Well, that sounds... lovely," I said.

"Oh, it was. Quite a wonderful way to end my time here."

"Can you cut the small talk? We're burning daylight here," Granny said. "I'm going to go see if Cheris is near the police station yet."

I fiddled with the amber ring on my finger. "Listen, Brigid. After you left yesterday, I tried to find you, obviously I wasn't successful, but um... I wanted to ask you about something."

She made a pout in the mirror, checking her teeth for lipstick. "Oh, all right. Go on then."

"The first time you came into the bookstore, you recognized a woman that works there. Heather?"

"Heather?" Brigid frowned. *Had Trixie been confused?* I wondered.

"Yeah, Heather. Kinda curvy, dark hair."

"Oh! Yes." Brigid threw the lipstick back in her purse and

pulled out a tube of mascara. "Except when I knew her, she went by Katie. Strange seeing her here."

"Yeah, she mentioned she changed her name." I paused. "How do you know her, anyway?"

"Oh, well she used to be a member of my coven." Brigid leaned forward and started flicking the mascara wand against her eyelashes, their natural pale color turning to black.

"Your coven?" But Heather's coven had been taken out by a witch hunter. I supposed it was possible that Heather had made a stop at another coven before settling in Blackwood Bay.

Brigid nodded. "Yes." She pumped the mascara wand in its tube.

"Heather said she came from a small coven in the middle of nowhere, Vermont." I was starting to grow suspicious of Brigid.

She barked out a laugh. "Not unless you count Phoenix as the middle of nowhere, Vermont." She waved her hand. "No, Katie grew up in my coven. Then one day she just up and disappeared. Always was a strange lass, that one, though."

No, that couldn't be right. Heather had said her entire coven was taken out by a witch hunter. I instinctively took a step back from Brigid and I could tell she sensed my nervousness. What if she really was the witch hunter Heather was so terrified of? She shoved the mascara wand back in its tube and turned to face me.

"Mind telling me what all these questions are about? I have a feeling you're trying to use my pieces to put together your own puzzle."

I studied Brigid for a moment. *If she was a witch hunter, wouldn't she just kill me right here on the spot? We are alone together in this bathroom. No witnesses.*

"Out with it then, lass. Tell me what's going on in that head of yours."

"Heather—er, Katie—said she came to Blackwood Bay because her coven was wiped out by a witch hunter."

Brigid erupted in laughter and I felt a bit embarrassed as I waited for her to stop. She wiped under her eyes, "No, certainly not." She chuckled again. "Oh, you're ruining the mascara I just applied!" She turned to the mirror to wipe under her eyes. "Our coven is still very much alive and well. As I said, Katie just up and left us one day. No note or anything."

"Weren't you all concerned about her?"

Brigid shrugged. "Katie was always an odd duck. Pushed back against the elders any chance she got. Never wanted much to do with any of us. Quite abrasive most of the time. None of us were very surprised that she'd gone. I don't think she cared for any of us much."

I was shocked. That did not sound like the Heather I knew. Except... I didn't really know her that well at all.

"Are you sure the woman you saw in the bookstore was this Katie person?"

Brigid turned to face me. "I may be old, but I am *not* senile, lass."

"She's coming! I see her barreling down Main Street! Hurry!" Granny appeared behind Brigid.

"Listen, I have to run. Sorry. Thanks, Brigid. Safe travels!" I called out over my shoulder as I hurried from the bathroom back out onto the street.

"Granny," I whispered, "she said Heather isn't really Heather. Her name is Katie and her coven is still very much alive. No witch hunter."

"No, that can't be right." Granny shook her head.

"Why would Brigid lie though?" I spotted Cheris bustling toward us, though she was busy talking on her cell phone, her head swiveling around in every direction like she was looking for someone.

"Maybe Heather's right. And maybe we were just in the company of a witch hunter ourselves." Granny said.

"Why wouldn't she have just killed me right there then? It makes no sense," I argued.

Granny shrugged. "Maybe she didn't want to dirty up that pristine bathroom. Anyway, we'll have to work it out later. We need to hurry." Granny was right; Cheris was going to beat us to the police station. I quickened my pace and she spotted me right as I approached the entrance of the police station. She froze and muttered something into her cell phone before dropping it down at her side.

It took her a moment too long, but she recovered, a fake smile plastered across her face as she adjusted her posture. "Well, hello there."

"Cheris." I nodded. "Funny running into you." I crossed my arms over my chest, refusing to make things easy for her.

"Mmm… yes. So what are you out doing today? Shouldn't you be over at the bookstore this time of morning?" she checked her wrist but there was no watch on it.

"Are you seriously going to try to make small talk? How about instead you tell me why your niece was pretending to be me? And why *you* pretended not to know about it?"

She narrowed her eyes and pursed her lips before grabbing me by the arm and dragging me into the small alleyway next to the police station.

"Ouch!" I ripped my arm away from her. She tried to regain her composure, smoothing the front of her charcoal-colored dress and running a hand over her still perfectly styled hair.

"I apologize." She clasped her hands together. "Listen, Dru, is it? Listen, Dru, I think there's been a bit of a misunder-standing."

I rolled my eyes. "Your family loves to use that phrase, but no, there hasn't."

"Look! None of this would've happened if your grand-mother hadn't been such a stubborn old hag!" She raised her voice.

"So you just killed her because she wouldn't sell it to you!" I shouted back.

"No!" She shook her head and put her hand to her mouth. "No, that's not what happened."

"Cheris, my grandmother was murdered. You wanted her building for your little empire. I just found out that your niece was my impostor. You acted like you'd never met her before in your life. You think that isn't all highly suspicious?"

"Listen," she hissed, "that all may be true. But I did *not* hurt Drusilla! I'm no murderer!"

"You really think I'm buying that? You want to know what I think?"

"Not really, no," she said, a vein throbbing in her neck.

"Tough. I think you killed Granny and planned on having your niece pose as me, have her sign the necessary documenta-tion to take ownership of the bookstore so she could hand it over to you. Just like you've always wanted."

She looked taken aback, "No. No that's not what happened! I didn't kill anyone!"

"What I can't figure out is how you managed to poison her cheesecake or why you'd kill Trixie and the lawyer. That was pretty stupid. You needed him alive to sign the documents. Was he threatening to out you? To go to the police?"

"What? *No*! I told you, I didn't kill anyone! All those deaths were related?" Cheris's eyes widened.

"Like you didn't know," I scoffed.

"No, no. I had no idea." She shook her head. "You—you said something about Drusilla's cheesecake being poisoned, right?"

I nodded.

"Listen, the day she died, I was at Peaches' picking up some croissants for a staff brunch. I saw Heather come in and pick up a box. Her and Peaches were talking about how it was for Granny. Heather left with it and I watched her walk straight back to the bookstore." Cheris raised her eyebrows. "Don't you see? It must've been Peaches!" She took a step toward me and lowered her voice as if to let me in on some big secret, "But why would she kill Drusilla?"

I thought for a moment. I knew the cheesecake had come from Peaches, but I didn't know Heather had come in and picked it up. She'd never mentioned that and neither had Granny. "Peaches didn't have any reason to want Granny dead. Unlike you." I knew that wasn't *entirely* true, but Cheris didn't.

"Dru, I didn't kill your grandmother. I didn't like her. That's no secret. I'm not particularly sorry that she's dead, either, if I'm being honest."

"Well, that's a first. Usually she's lying like a no-legged dog." Granny snorted.

Cheris continued, "But I didn't kill her. I simply tried to take advantage of the fact that she had died. That's not a crime."

"No, but forging documents is," I replied.

"No documents were forged. Nothing illegal has occurred."

I wasn't sure if I was buying it. But Cheris would've surely been noticed if she'd been inside the bookstore that day. As much as I hated to admit it, I sort of believed her.

"I'm still going to tell the police what you were up to," I said.

"I know." She studied me for a moment before pulling her wallet from her purse. She rifled around in it for a moment before handing me a stack of one hundred dollar bills.

Reading the confusion on my face she said, "Buy yourself a new car."

If I were in a cartoon, a lightbulb would've lit up over my head. "Wait... did you have my car and the first rental car stolen?"

Cheris shook her head. "Absolutely not. I simply hired someone to keep tabs on you. So I would know exactly when to expect you. I overheard Mitch saying that you'd be arriving in town after you had your affairs in order. You're quite earlier than anticipated, by the way. Anyway, if the man I hired chose to participate in nefarious activities, I certainly had no part in that. And I don't conduct business in that manner, of course."

I sneered. "So you only participate in white-collar crimes then?"

"As I said, no crimes were committed by me. However, I do feel slightly responsible that you are without transportation possibly due to someone who I hired. I obviously misjudged him. So I would like to give you a peace offering."

"Are you trying to buy my silence or what?"

She shook her head. "No. I would just like us to get off on a better foot."

"I'm still not selling. And if I ever do decide to sell, you are the last person on earth that I would consider." I spun around and left her standing alone in the alleyway.

"I think she's telling the truth, Granny," I whispered.

"I hate to say it, but I think she is too."

"We have to consider Peaches again."

Granny began to protest.

"I know... I know. But what other explanation is there?"

"Wait!" I turned and ran back toward the police station, catching Cheris just as she opened the door.

"Cheris!"

She turned to face me.

"You said you saw Heather go into Peaches' and pick up cheesecake for Granny."

She nodded.

"Did you hear anything they said? Was it a strange interaction or did Peaches seem normal to you?"

Cheris thought for a moment, "No, she seemed like her usual tacky self."

"Did you overhear their conversation? Did she say anything about the cheesecake?"

"Well, she certainly didn't say it was poisoned."

"No, of course not. But did she say anything else? Please try to think. It might be important."

Cheris nodded. "They were talking about how she was trying out new recipes in preparation for the upcoming fall season. I saw her place it in the box. A grotesque orange-hued thing."

"Orange?" That struck me as odd. "Did you hear her say what kind it was?"

"No," Cheris drew the word out slowly as if she were still thinking. "Oh, wait! I do remember! She said it was pumpkin."

"Pumpkin? Are you sure?"

"Yes, definitely pumpkin." Cheris nodded emphatically.

Peaches had made Granny pumpkin cheesecake. *Not* cherry coffee. Which means someone switched out Peaches' version for the deadly one.

CHAPTER 19

I pulled my phone from my pocket and texted Heather:

What kind of cheesecake did Peaches make Granny?

"If Heather can confirm what Cheris said, then we know for sure that Peaches didn't do this," I told Granny.

"I already know she didn't," Granny said.

Pumpkin, I think? I do remember that it was orange. Heather texted back.

Thanks. Someone switched them out. Peaches didn't poison Granny. Are you alone?

No. Tilly is here with me. Do you think it could be the witch hunter?

I typed a quick reply: *I really don't know. Just be careful.*

"Heather confirmed it. Peaches didn't make the one that killed you. Someone for sure switched them out. Where you in the bookstore all day?"

"Mostly."

"Was anyone unusual in? Or someone that might've had a reason to do this?"

"Not that I remember."

"Do you think there really could be a witch hunter here?" I asked, a shiver running up my spine. "Maybe Brigid isn't really Brigid. Maybe she was lying."

"She has to be, Dru. There has to be more to this."

"Crap. So I really could've died in that bathroom." I hurried into the bookstore, locking the door behind me. "I wish there were curtains in this place," I muttered.

"Just do a cloaking spell," Granny said.

"I don't know how." I locked the door behind me. "Wait, I saw Heather with a book of spells the other day... where did she put it?" I said more to myself then to Granny.

"Hiya!?" Trixie's voice pierced the silence in the room.

"Trixie, hey. Did you find the dog?"

She nodded. "Yup, took me awhile. He's at that cute cop's house."

Harper was keeping Mitch's dog? "Really?"

"Yup. Such a sweet thing. And so friendly! Wish I could've brought him home with me."

"Okay, good work, Trixie," I said.

"I should text Harper and let him know about my conversation with Cheris." I pulled out my phone.

"Trixie, do you remember who came into the store the day I died?"

Granny and I made eye contact, knowing it was a long shot that Trixie would remember.

Trixie looked thoughtful. "You, me, Heather, Dorothy-"

"Dorothy?" I asked.

Trixie nodded.

"Maybe we need to talk about her too."

Granny shook her head. "No way. Dorothy would never hurt me. And she certainly wouldn't have done a thing to Trixie."

"Maybe not, but what if it was the witch hunter *pretending* to be Dorothy?"

"That's a possibility." Granny nodded.

"This is getting confusing." Trixie wandered off, twirling a pigtail.

"Here's what I don't understand. Why would he off you and Trixie in such an … uneventful fashion?" I asked.

"How would you like him to do it, Dru?" Granny raised an eyebrow.

"I just mean you hear 'witch hunter' and you think like, some sword-wielding guy creeping around looking for witches. Not a dude who poisons desserts."

Granny nodded. "It's actually pretty smart, if you think about it. Getting rid of us one-by-one in ways that can't draw any attention to himself. Wait until we're alone and vulnerable and unsuspecting."

I shrugged. "I guess. Heather said the witch hunter that attacked her coven was pretty violent though. That is, if she's even telling the truth."

"What do you mean?" Trixie asked from a seat she'd taken on the floor.

"I mean, we don't know for sure and Heather could very well be lying."

"Unless that Irish broad is a witch hunter. One of them has to be lying," Granny said.

"Right. Which brings back the question of why she didn't just kill me when she had me alone today."

"You were in a public place, for one. For two, maybe you aren't high on the list."

"Except that now she probably thinks I suspect her, since I questioned her."

"You need to work on your magic. If there is a witch hunter

in town, you're in danger."

"Granny, there's a *killer* in town. Regardless of their species, I think I'm already in danger."

～

"*Y*ou are actually really terrible at this." Granny stood with her arms across her chest.

"Hey, I got the cloaking spell to work, didn't I?" I argued.

"No, she's right. You're dreadful," Maui chimed in. He'd joined us down in the bookstore as if I needed a third to judge my magic skills, or lack thereof.

I groaned. "I'm going to be like Minnie, aren't I? Serving people worm-filled chimichangas." I flopped down on the couch and yawned, glancing at the huge clock on the wall. "I'm tired and it's already after nine. We've been at this all day. Maybe we can try again tomorrow." I couldn't help but feel a bit defeated. Using my magic was much tougher than I'd expected. Movies always make it look so easy, but being a real life witch is hard work.

Maui caught me checking my cell phone. "Waiting for a call?"

"Yeah. I thought Harper might get in touch after he talked with Tiffany but I haven't heard from him yet. Kinda strange."

A loud thud came from the glass front door and I jumped. I walked toward it, thankful that whoever was out there couldn't see in. Regardless, I crept slowly up to the door until I saw that it was Harper. I felt a wave of both relief and giddiness rush over me as I fumbled to unlock the door.

"Good thing he can't see you tripping all over yourself to let him in," Granny mumbled.

I took a second before opening the door to smooth my hair and adjust my top.

I casually opened it to his back and he spun around to face me. A broad smile spread across his face. "Hey."

"Hi." I smiled. "I've been waiting to hear from you."

"Oh?" he raised his eyebrows.

"Yeah, after you took Tiffany in for questioning?"

"Oh, right." His cheeks flushed slightly.

"Come in." I led him into the bookstore and took a seat on the stool behind the counter. I wasn't sure why but having the glass countertop between us made me feel less vulnerable.

"I came bearing gifts." He held out a small paper bag.

"Aww, you shouldn't have." I could feel a goofy smile forming on my face as I took it from him. I could feel his eyes on me as I unrolled the top of the bag and stuck my hand inside.

"A bell?" The shiny silver bell made a tinkling noise as I pulled it out.

"Yeah. For the front door." He motioned.

"But how did you know I wanted a bell for the door?" I was certain I'd never told him that.

He winked and took it from my hand before fixing it to the door handle. I felt a wave of uneasiness creeping up inside me for the first time in his presence. I was sure I'd never mentioned to him that I wanted a bell for the door. How did he know?

I watched him finish messing with the bell's wire before he locked the door. "I know you had a little chat with Cheris Sterling today." He turned to me, changing the subject.

I nodded, still slightly stunned.

"Well, for the record, they pretty much spilled everything. Turns out, after Granny passed, Cheris asked Mitch Powders about buying this place. She wanted to know what was going to happen to the building after Drusilla died and he said it was being left to her granddaughter. He told her to take up her request to purchase with you but that you wouldn't be in town for at least a few weeks. That's when she came up with the brilliant plan to have Tiffany pretend to be you and have the building signed over to her. She offered to give Tiffany a huge chunk of cash in return. Then you showed up and ruined everything." He teased.

"I tend to do that," I joked, but my voice was unsteady.

"No. No, I don't think you do," he said quietly, his eyes lingering on mine a little too long. "I know my world got a whole lot more exciting once you arrived."

I felt my stomach flip and fought the heat that would inevitably be rushing to my cheeks. "Well, if you count murders and fraud to be exciting." I tried to shrug off his comment.

An unexpected vibration came from my back pocket and I slipped out my phone to check who was calling. Tilly.

"Hello?"

"Dru! Thank God you answered! Where are you?" It was Heather.

"I'm at the bookstore. Why are you calling from Tilly's phone?"

"Mine is dead. Listen! You know that hot cop?" Heather said.

I rolled my eyes, hoping he couldn't hear her through the phone.

"We saw him shapeshift!" Heather's voice was hurried.

"Wait, what does that mean?" I asked, rapidly pushing the button on the side of my phone to lower the volume.

"Dru! I saw him shapeshift! He's the witch hunter!"

CHAPTER 20

"Oh." A wave of dread washed over me and I felt my stomach drop. "Okay. Um, listen, I have to go because Sergeant Harper just stopped by." I was hoping she would get the hint that I was in imminent danger.

"Oh my god, Dru! Okay, Tilly and I are on our way. We'll call Dorothy and Peaches on our way over. Just stall him, okay?" Heather said.

"Okay, sounds great. Thanks." My voice trembled.

"Everything okay?" Harper asked as I slid my phone back into my pocket.

"Yeah, great. Heather called out sick today so she was just checking in." I lied.

"Is your dad still in town?" Harper leaned his elbow on the counter.

"My dad?"

He nodded.

"How did you know my dad was here?" There it was, that sinking dread again.

"Chief Carver and I ran into him," Harper said, his voice so casual, as if he wasn't here to kill me. I tried to sneak a look at Granny, but she was busy whispering with Trixie.

"Oh." I avoided his question. Harper studied me intently for a moment and I wasn't sure if he wanted to kiss me or kill me. Maybe both. I needed to buy time until my cavalry arrived.

I tried to catch Granny's eyes again, hoping desperately that she could read my mind, but suddenly she and Trixie both disappeared. Oh my God, of all the times I'd wanted those two to leave me alone and they choose to do it at the worst possible time. Figures. I really needed to peek at the Spell Book. Maybe there was something in there I could use to at least buy some time. I could really use it right about now.

"So aside from the murders and people trying to run you out of town, how are you liking it here?" Harper asked. He leaned further onto the counter and I was thankful for the glass countertop between us. It wouldn't do much to protect me if he tried to attack me, but it made me feel less exposed somehow.

"Uh, it's great," I managed.

"Are you sure everything's okay?" He furrowed his brow and I let my eyes meet his. They were truly the bluest I'd ever seen and they seemed so kind. I cursed myself for misreading a man yet again. Turns out this one didn't just want to break my heart: he actually wanted to kill me.

"Everything's fine. I just need some water," I rasped. He righted himself suddenly and I jumped. He gave me a confused look before heading to the small refrigerator and pulling out a bottle of water for me. How sweet. He didn't want me to die parched.

Granny and Trixie had deserted me, but I knew Heather and Tilly were at least on their way. I had no clue when he planned to strike and I doubted I could take him down by myself. I needed to buy more time.

I gave a quick scan to the area around me. I caught the gold lettering of the Spell Book shining at me from a shelf under the countertop. I needed to knock him out. That's what they do in movies, right?

Harper handed me the water, his fingers brushing mine and I felt the familiar butterflies in my stomach. *Really, Dru? This man wants you dead and you're still getting butterflies over him?* I had the fear sweats and my damp, shaky hand dropped the water bottle. I watched it roll across the floor, stopping when it hit Harper's shoe. He bent to pick it up and that's when I had my now-or-never moment.

I searched for something heavy to hit him over the head with, but the nearest thing I saw was a glass vase behind him. Shoot. There was no way I could get to it. He stood, extending his hand to me again, when suddenly his head lurched forward and I watched his eyes roll back into his head before he crumpled to the ground.

I shrieked and the heavy glass vase fell behind him, smashing into pieces. Oh my God—I'd managed to hit him over the head with it without even touching it. Gah, it never worked quite the way I wanted it to, but score one point for magic! I felt my hands trembling, but I needed to get him tied up fast.

"Good Lord, woman! What has gotten into you?" Maui leaped onto the countertop.

"Help me find something to tie him up with," I wheezed, my hands under Harper's armpits as I tried to drag all two hundred and some odd pounds of him out from behind the counter.

Maui dashed away and I collapsed onto the carpeted floor. Over the sound of my gasps for air, I heard the clinking of keys against the glass door. I couldn't have been more relieved to see Heather's face.

"Oh my God! Are you okay?" She ran to me, dropping to her knees beside me.

I nodded, still trying to catch my breath. "I managed to knock him out, but we need to tie him up." Heather jumped up and ran to the back room. I kept a close eye on Harper and noticed he was drooling. As angry as I was, I was relieved that he was still alive. I wanted answers.

Heather came up next to me, a bundle of rope in her hands. "Help me drag him to the sitting area," she said. "I don't think we'll be able to lift him onto the couch, but we can at least sit him upright so we can tie his hands and feet."

I did as instructed, grabbing one of his arms as Heather grabbed the other. Even knocked out, his biceps felt like rocks and I shook the thought away. This wasn't the man I thought he was. The one who had maybe kind of liked me. It was someone who wanted me dead.

"Where's Tilly?" I asked.

"Oh," Heather panted, "she went to get Dorothy, Minnie, and Peaches."

"So you came here all alone?" I was shocked. As terrified as Heather had seemed of the witch hunter, here she was.

"I couldn't let you face him alone." She heaved. "Are Granny and Trixie here?"

"No, they disappeared after you called earlier. Wish I knew where'd they'd run off to." We reached the couch and I collapsed with Harper's arm across my stomach.

"We'd better get him tied up before he wakes," Heather said, gasping for air.

"Wait." A thought occurred to me. "What if there really is a Harper and the witch hunter just shapeshifted into him? And that's what you saw? What if this really is an innocent man?" I pushed Harper's arm off of me.

Heather looked thoughtful for a moment. "I really don't think that's the case, Dru."

"But why?" I was desperately hanging on to the hope that there was an explanation that left Harper innocent of any wrongdoing.

"Because I saw him shapeshift from the Irish woman into himself."

"But that still doesn't mean—"

"Have you looked very closely at the eyes?"

"The eyes?" I asked.

"Yes, the one thing shapeshifters can't change about themselves is their eyes." So that's why my father's eyes were so familiar to me when he was running around as the man in the shark hat. I knew every time I'd seen Harper, his eyes were that same brilliant blue. They were striking and impossible to mistake. But I hadn't paid any attention to Brigid's eyes. Wouldn't I have noticed if they were the same as Harper's?

"I didn't notice Brigid's—the Irish woman's—eyes," I said.

"Well, I did. The day she came into the store and tried to scare me by calling me Katie. They were very blue. What color are Harper's eyes?" Heather leaned forward to lift one of his closed eyelids. She gasped and fell back against the couch. "Dru, it's the same person. I swear it."

I felt my lip trembling and I knew I was on the verge of tears. "What do we do now?"

"Let's tie him up and wait for the others to get here." I followed Heather's lead in silence, and I could feel Maui's eyes on me as I worked.

"We should probably tape his mouth too," Heather said. "I'm going to run to the back room and see what I can find. Will you be okay?"

I nodded and my eyes met Maui's.

"You really liked him, eh?" Maui leaped onto the couch next to Harper and perched next to his lolling head.

"I did." A small laugh escaped me. "I sure know how to pick 'em, don't I?"

"Uh, hello?" A man's voice broke the silence and I spun around to see Mitch Powders standing near the front door. "Sorry for... interrupting? Is everything all right?" He had a horrified look on his face as he peered around me at Harper.

"I didn't think I'd see you again." I ignored his question.

"I wasn't planning on it, but, well, some of my memories finally came back and I needed to pay you a visit. I don't have much time, so I need to make this quick."

"Wow. Well, thank you, Mitch, but I think I got most of it figured out. I don't think the murders were related to your involvement, actually. I do know Cheris Sterling played a large role. She wouldn't admit it, but she paid you off, didn't she?"

Mitch shook his head violently. "No. No, it wasn't Cheris at all. Remember I told you I thought I was supposed to meet someone on the beach that night? Well, I was. Her whole plan was to get me out there to kill me so I couldn't tell anyone the truth. You were right—your Granny never had a will or a living trust made."

He spoke in a hurried tone. "But she—she came into my office and said I had to make one and she even forged Granny's signature. I think she had some weird power or something. Like mind control? I don't know, but she said some words out loud and then it was like I *had* to do what she said. I had no choice."

"Mitch!" I interrupted him, my voice louder than I intended. "Who is 'she?'"

Mitch's eyes darted around the room. "Heather."

CHAPTER 21

"*H*eather?" I choked out.

"Yes?" I saw Heather standing in front of the tie-dye curtain, a roll of duct tape in her hand.

I froze.

She walked toward me, glancing over at Harper as she went. "Who are you talking to out here?"

"No, that doesn't make any sense." I shook my head.

"It's true." Mitch held up his hands, "It was her. It was her at my office that day, and it was her at the beach that night. She killed me. Get to a phone and call the police. She's no friend," Mitch said and then, poof, he was gone.

"What doesn't make any sense?" Heather looked around. "What's going on?"

I felt my heart thudding in my chest. Heather set up the living trust? Heather killed Mitch?

"Heather, I need to ask you something."

She offered me a blank stare.

"Did you—did you go to Mitch Powders to set up Granny's living trust?" In retrospect, I shouldn't have asked. I should've kept that tidbit of information to myself. But my mind was reeling, and I just wanted answers.

Heather's eyes widened. "What? Why would you think that?"

"Because that's what he told me."

She shook her head. "No way. It was obviously the witch hunter pretending to be me."

I nodded and eased myself back behind the counter. I needed her to think I believed her, though I wasn't sure yet whether I did or not. "Okay. Maybe there's a spell to bind him from shifting?"

"There might be," Heather said, but I could see the suspicion in her eyes.

"I'll check the Spell Book." I pulled it out from under the counter and began flipping through the pages, my mind unable to focus. All of a sudden, the book seemed to take on a life of its own, the pages flying rapidly until they fell flat on a page containing a small purple bookmark wedged deep inside the binding. In bold cursive lettering at the top of the page were the words: **INCANTATION TO TAKE POSSESSION OF ANOTHER'S MAGIC**

Oh my God, what?! Why would there be a bookmark in this of all pages? This was like that dark witch stuff that Eve had been talking about. Who was reading this last? And in an instant, the puzzle pieces all fell into place, just as I felt something come down hard on the back of my head.

~

I could see light through my closed eyelids. They felt too heavy to open and my head pounded. I tried to raise my arm to touch my head, but realized it was tied to something. I could feel the warmth of a body next to me and realized I must be lying next to Harper. I was too afraid to open my eyes.

"I know you're awake." Heather's voice came from close by. I willed myself to open my eyes and saw her sitting across from me in the velvet tufted chair, her legs crossed and the roll of duct tape dangling from one hand.

She chuckled. "I was hoping to do this a little more symbolically, but I guess this works too."

My throat burned and I felt Harper groan beside me. I silently begged him to wake up.

"Kind of funny that you knocked out the one person who could've saved you." She snickered.

"That's because I trusted you!" I rasped. "You told me he was a witch hunter and I believed you. I thought you were my friend."

She threw her head back and burst into a fit of laughter. Admittedly, that stung.

"Oh, God, no. I never wanted to be your friend. You're sort of helpless, you know that? Even if I didn't want to kill you and steal your magic, I still wouldn't have been your friend."

Ouch. "So you're a dark witch? You really did kill Granny and Trixie?"

"Obviously." She rolled her eyes. "Granny had to go first because you'd inherit her magic. She got her cheesecake from Peaches every week like clockwork. It was easy enough to make one with ground-up cherry pits in the crust and then just swap it out with the one Peaches had made. I had hoped it would look like the old witch had just had a heart attack, but I guess I went a little overboard." She shrugged and gave me a half smile.

"And then I had to find a way to get you here. Granny was just the sacrificial lamb. Then I realized she'd never made a will, so I had to take care of that little matter as well. A mind control spell on Mitch Powders. Simple enough. It was all going quite seamlessly too until that stupid cow Brigid showed up and recognized me in front of Trixie. I mean, we all know Trixie's an idiot, but I couldn't risk the chance that she'd say something about it to someone and they'd start nosing around. Just like you did. So I had to kill her too. Ground up cherry pits in a homemade tea bag that I switched out with one of hers. You know, it's actually quite scary how easily you can find ways to kill people on the internet." Heather chuckled.

"So your coven never was killed, were they? Brigid was telling the truth."

"Oh, definitely. That was a big fat lie I told you. There never was a witch hunter. I just needed to throw the scent off of my trail long enough to get what I wanted. Then I was going to ride off into the sunset. I already have my bags packed and everything."

"Did you hurt Tilly?"

Heather waved her hand. "Nah. Just gave her a heavy dose of sleeping meds mixed in with her tea. I mean, what kind of a person do you think I am? I'm not killing for sport!" She stood and paced in front of me.

"Where's Granny?" She spun around.

"She's not here." That was the truth. Granny had ditched me.

Heather knelt in front of me and her eyes seared into mine. "Okay," she said in a low voice, decidedly believing me. She stood and pulled the Spell Book from the table next to her and began pacing again.

"Now, I've never done this before, so you'll have to bear with me. I didn't plan on making your death painful, but now that you know the truth, I doubt you'll eat or drink anything I give you, so..." she shrugged and made a quick grab for Harper's gun. He startled and I saw his eyes flutter open.

"Dru," he mumbled.

"Are you okay?" I whispered, "We need to do something quick or we're both dead."

He made a grunting noise, his eyes rolling back in his head again, and I realized he'd been rendered useless. This was on me. A witch who didn't really know how to use her magic.

Heather turned abruptly toward me. "I bind you—"

"Wait, you *bind* me? What does that mean? You bind me from what?"

"I bind you—" she started again.

"Yeah, I know, from what though?"

"I *bind* you—" she said more firmly, ignoring me.

"Wait, are you doing a curse? Like putting a hex on me or whatever?"

Heather gave an exasperated groan before she made her way toward me, tearing off a strip of duct tape from the roll. I kicked at her as she approached, trying to buy as much time as I could, but for what I wasn't exactly sure. I heard a high-pitched snarl and Maui pounced on her back. She let out a throaty sound before getting ahold of him and throwing him to the ground.

"Bloody wanker!" Maui exclaimed.

Heather cursed as my heel connected with her arm. "I have to bind you from doing magic first!" she yelled.

"Why are you doing this? Why do you want to steal my magic?" I knew the answer. It was simple. But I hoped I could keep her talking long enough to come up with a plan.

Heather gave an exasperated sigh. "You don't even deserve it, you know that? You have no idea how much power you have and you have no idea how to use it. It's embarrassing, really."

"So you want to kill me and take it for yourself because I don't know how to use it?"

"No," she hissed, "I want to kill you and take it because I want that power. I was born to a weak line. I'm barely capable of doing much at all without a Spell Book. It's not fair. But you —you have this great magic just given to you and it's being wasted. I deserve it! Not you!"

She shoved a piece of duct tape over my mouth. "Now shut up and let me finish what I've started."

CHAPTER 22

*O*h, God. This was it. This was how I was going to die. Where the heck was my Guardian, anyway? Wasn't he supposed to be keeping me safe? And here I was, about to meet my demise. A thought occurred to me: maybe Granny had gone to find him. Surely, she must have. She wouldn't just desert me. I silently pleaded for someone, anyone to come save me. I elbowed Harper as hard as I could, willing him to wake up.

"I bind you—" Heather started again and without warning, the warmth of Harper's presence next to me vanished. I turned to look, but he was gone. The rope that had been around his hands and feet lay on the floor, knots still tied. I looked to Heather and saw the shock on her face.

"Where'd he go?" She raced over to me and ripped the duct tape from my mouth. I cried out. *Guess I won't need to get a wax anytime soon.*

"What did you do? Where is he?" She shouted, spinning around to look for him.

"Nothing. I don't know where he went." I searched the room

for him, but he was gone. I looked to Maui, whose eyes were trailing something.

"Did you see?" I asked him, my eyes following his gaze up to a bee buzzing angrily as it made a nosedive for Heather.

She cursed and batted at it.

"Now is not the time to be distracted," I whispered to Maui.

"Amazing," was all he replied with.

Heather's shriek pierced my ears and I turned to see her hand on the back of her neck. "It stung me!" She looked at me as if I cared.

"I'm allergic!" she said, as if that made a difference either, and ran to the back room.

This was my chance! I struggled hard against the ropes around my wrists, closing my eyes from the pain. I felt a presence next to me, and expecting to see Heather, I leaned away, but when I opened my eyes, they found Harper's face. His brow creased as he worked on untying my rope.

"Harper... What in the world? Where did you go?" I stammered.

"I can't really explain right now. We need to get you free," he rasped.

Maui started to say something, but I heard rustling coming from the back of the bookstore and knew Heather was on her way back out.

"Hurry. Please," I pleaded.

"Ah, you're back." I heard Heather's voice as she raised the gun at Harper, but it was drowned out by a loud banging. My hands free of the rope, I bolted up next to Harper as a posse of glorious witches came hastily piling through the front door. I could feel the tears of relief welling in my eyes as I saw Dorothy, Minnie, Peaches, Astra, and Electra. I looked to Heather's direction, but she had disappeared.

"I brought back-up." The sound of Granny's voice filled the room and the tears began to flow easily.

"Granny! I thought you deserted me," I sobbed.

"Not a chance. Do you have any idea how long it takes to communicate with people who can't see or hear ghosts? I went to Eve's first, tried spelling out a message with the magnetic letters on her refrigerator, but her kid kept taking them to spell out words like 'poop' and 'butt.' Little scamp."

"But how did you know?" I choked out.

"I heard your phone call and you asked why she was calling from Tilly's phone. It didn't make much sense to me that Tilly wouldn't have just called herself. Something just didn't feel right. I decided to take a quick trip to check things out and found Tilly passed out in an armchair. I had a Saint Bernard that didn't even drool that much. Anyway, if she knew you were in danger, Tilly wouldn't have decided that it was a good time for a nap. That's when I knew." Granny turned and narrowed her eyes in Heather's direction.

Harper took a step forward, holding his arm out in front of me like a human seatbelt.

"Well, where is she?" Dorothy had a frightening look on her face, her lips curled in anger.

"I'm gonna jerk her bald! She's done nothin' but lie to us— peein' on our backs and tellin' us it's rainin'!" Peaches' cheeks were red and she shook her fist as her daughters stifled their laughter.

"Did you all call the police?" I asked weakly.

"This isn't a matter for the police." Dorothy shook her head.

"Shut up! All of you!" I heard Heather's voice coming from behind a bookshelf near the back of the store. "You all really should've stayed home and minded your own business. Now I'm going to have to kill each and every one of you."

"We're not afraid of you. Your magic is mediocre at best," Dorothy shouted back, but her voice faltered just enough that I felt panic creeping its way back in.

"I don't need it to get rid of you." She held the gun steady over the top of the shelf, pointing it at the huddle of witches. "I came here to steal Rathmore magic, and I'm not leaving until I do."

"Wow. Not cool, Heather," Electra said, folding her arms over her chest.

"Yeah, it's really not," Astra chimed in, flipping a pink strand of hair from her shoulder.

I heard whispering coming from behind the bookshelf and Heather stumbled out a moment later, her face already red and puffy from the bee sting. Dorothy promptly raised her hand and I watched confusion overtake her previous confidence. She pulled her hand back and shoved it forward a bit more forcefully, but nothing seemed to happen.

Peaches shouldered her way to the front of the group and steadied herself before closing her eyes and taking in a deep breath. She gave an agonizingly slow exhale before opening them.

"But…" was all she said, astonished.

I heard murmuring and a sly smile spread across Heather's swelling face.

"Protection spell." She shrugged, lifting the gun. "Now, which one of you wants to go first?"

"Ew, what's wrong with your face?" Astra asked.

Harper gently pushed me back with his arm.

"Bee sting." Heather raised her hand and touched her cheek, I could see the swelling intensify, her eyes becoming nothing more than slits. She looked terrifying.

"None of you has to die if you just give me what I want."

She soldiered on, "Well, no one other than Dru, anyway. Why don't you all just go home and pretend like you were never here?" Heather waved the gun around.

"I need you to get down behind the couch," Harper whispered to me.

"No, please," I whispered back. The last thing I wanted was him to die trying to be a hero.

"Too late," he mumbled and I stood in stunned silence as he changed from a man into a large, silver-furred wolf. It was quite fitting actually, given his name. His change was punctuated by the sound of gasps. Mine included.

"Wait. He really *is* a shapeshifter?" Heather's voice shook as she turned the gun on Harper. I imagined her eyes would've grown wide if they'd been able to.

"Is—is there really a witch hunter here too?" I asked, suddenly terrified again of this man-wolf that I had thought was trying to save me. My body froze in place. I heard a low growl coming from Harper and for a brief moment his eyes met mine. It was definitely him; his piercing eyes were unmistakable.

"You can't be serious?" Granny groaned. "He's not a witch hunter, idiot. He's your Guardian."

"My Guardian?" I whispered. *Harper was my Guardian? Oh, how could I have missed it?* Granny was right; I was an idiot.

"He's your Guardian?" Heather repeated, as if she were trying to wrap her mind around the words.

"Well, then he definitely has to die." I heard her cock the gun and suddenly everything felt like it was happening in slow motion. Harper leaped through the air, a guttural sound coming from him, and I saw Heather's hand jerk back, a silver bullet escaping the cylinder. I felt something like a scream come from my body and I instinctively raised my hand.

It was in that moment that I saw a brilliant shine coming from the amber stone in my ring. Light was moving within it as if it were alive and I felt a jolt of something like electricity. A sudden rush of heat traveled through every inch of my body. Between my fingers, I watched the bullet that had been traveling directly toward Harper drop straight to the ground.

Time seemed to pick up its usual pace again, and Wolf Harper's paws hit the ground for the briefest moment before he tackled Heather.

I wasn't exactly sure what had just happened and I looked to my coven, but they simply stood with mouths agape, staring at the bullet on the ground.

"You did it!" I heard Granny's excitement.

"I bind you—" I heard Heather starting again as she struggled against Harper.

"Dru, do something!" Peaches yelled.

"What? Why me?"

"Because she has a protection spell around her. Our magic won't work!" Dorothy shouted over Harper's growls.

"I—I don't know what to do!" I said panicked.

I did the first thing I could think of—still used to using my human means—and ran and picked up the gun, my hands shaking.

"I can't just shoot her!" I shouted.

Harper had turned back into a man now and had pinned Heather to the ground as she grunted, struggling against him.

"If only I had thumbs!" Maui said.

"I'll do it!" Dorothy bellowed.

"Do something! Hurry!" Granny urged.

Before I could make a decision, Heather was up, having given Harper a knee to the groin, and she ran past me up the staircase to the apartment.

"Where is she going?" Astra asked.

"She knows I keep a gun up there," Granny said.

"Gun." I answered before turning to follow Heather.

"Don't!" Harper shouted. "There's no way I'm letting you go." He ripped his gun from my hands and ran past me. "Stay here," he commanded.

Yeah, right. I bounded up the steps behind him, and I could hear the footfalls of everyone else behind me.

I burst through the entryway of the apartment to the sound of my mother and Trixie both in a frenzy. Harper stood in the middle of the room, his gun drawn as he looked around. I felt bodies slamming into me from behind.

"If she's using a protection spell, why doesn't she just use her magic on us? Why does she need a gun?" I whispered.

"She can't use it to kill all of us. She's not strong enough," Peaches whispered back.

"Can't we break the spell?" I asked.

"It will wear off soon. That's why she's desperate to get rid of us first."

A gunshot rang out and I saw Harper hit the floor. Instinctively, I started to run to him when Heather's voice came from the staircase.

"Don't move!" she yelled. I stopped and turned to face her. She moved slowly across the living room, her gun taking turns between being pointed at me and everyone else. She stopped when she'd reached the kitchen, keeping her back to the row of front windows, certain no one could come up on her from behind.

"On the couch, all of you! I'm done playing games!" She waved the gun and everyone bustled past me onto the couch. I heard Harper moan and I looked down, unsure where he'd been shot.

"Kick the gun over here," Heather said. I looked at the gun on the floor and weighed my options. She had a protection spell around her, but I was able to stop the bullet earlier from hitting Harper. Maybe my magic was strong enough to overpower her.

"Now!" she barked. I touched the gun with the tip of my sneaker, desperately trying to think of what to do next.

"I bind you from doing magic," she began.

"Stop her, Dru!" my mother called out.

"Ugh. This again? You're really screwed this up, you know," I said.

"What did you say?" Heather spat.

"I mean, you had this master plan and at the very end, when it mattered most, you totally botched it. I don't think you'll make a very good dark witch, honestly." I crossed my arms over my chest, deciding I wasn't going to kick her the gun. If she was going to kill me, she'd have to work for it.

"I didn't botch anything! It's just a slight deviation from my original plan. It's fine." Her voice wavered.

"Eh, I mean, whatever you need to say to convince yourself. Granted, I don't know much about dark witches, but I imagine they're pretty diabolical. Calculated. Clever. And here you are waving a gun around at a room full of your peers. A gun? Really? I would expect, I don't know—maybe like, you in a creepy black cloak wandering around a candlelit room and chanting in some ancient language. Maybe I've watched too many movies, but I'm kind of disappointed, to be honest."

"Well, that was what was supposed to happen! I even have my cloak in my bag downstairs! But you ruined it. Talking to ghosts and snooping around in the Spell Book. Now we have to do things the hard way."

I laughed. "You're blaming me? What kind of absolute amateur leaves a bookmark in the page that details how to steal someone else's magic? Like I said, you're definitely not dark witch material."

"How dare you!" she seethed, rage burning in the little bits of her eyes that were still visible. She lunged at me unexpectedly and I instinctively raised my hands to protect myself. I caught a glimpse of my amber ring, its shine almost blinding as its various hues snaked around each other.

Behind it, I could see Heather's face, her mouth open in horror and I realized she wasn't coming any closer to me. In fact, she was flying backward. Farther and farther. While a wave of heat rushed through my body again, I realized that I was pushing her back. She flew through the glass window pane, its shattering sound almost deafening and a sickening thud came seconds later.

I stood staring at the fragmented window in shock as I felt a comforting arm come around my shoulders. Dorothy and Minnie blew past me, peering out the fractured window onto the concrete below.

I held my breath for what seemed like an eternity before Dorothy finally broke the silence. "Well, dear, you might want to put out an ad for *two* new employees."

CHAPTER 23

"This is the most delicious thing I've ever eaten in my life." My dad was nearly inhaling his third piece of strawberry cheesecake.

"It takes a special kind of bonehead to bring that into my house and eat it in front of me. He's lucky I'm not alive. I'd give him diarrhea for a month," Granny muttered to herself as she crossed the kitchen and gazed at the black tarp still covering the broken window.

"I'm sure it's just hard for him to remember you're here, since he can't see you." My mother fluttered her wings.

"Still making excuses for him nearly thirty years later," Granny grumbled.

"Granny's mad you brought cheesecake over," I said.

"Does she want a piece?" He grinned.

"Chump," Granny said.

"Dad, stop. You know that's what killed her."

"I know, but Peaches makes the best cheesecake in the world. I couldn't come into town and not pick one up. Besides, it wasn't *hers* that killed Granny."

"I don't think that's as relevant as you think it is." I rolled my eyes.

"All right. Sorry, Granny," my dad mumbled through a mouthful of cheesecake.

I fidgeted with the amber ring on my finger, still amazed that I'd been completely unaware that I was carrying around this magical piece of jewelry my whole life. My family explained to me that the ring itself didn't actually do anything; it just acted as sort of a supercharger to enhance my natural abilities. Granny said that it would only work for me, because I'm a lineal descendant and the one that's supposed to have it. Thinking about how careless I'd been as a child, I could've easily lost it and the thought made me grimace.

"Are you all right?" My dad interrupted my thoughts.

"I am. Thank you for turning around and coming back so quickly. I'm really glad you're here," I said, leaning back against the couch to rest my head next to a sleeping Maui. He'd made it back to Blackwood Bay in record time after Chief Carver had called and told him what happened. It had been roughly thirty-six hours since Heather had died trying to kill me, and I was still reeling from the experience.

He waved his hand. "No thanks necessary, sweetheart. There's no way I wasn't coming back after I found out what happened."

"I know. Still. Thank you."

"Any word on Wolf Harper?" he asked.

I shook my head. "He was asleep when I tried to visit him at the hospital yesterday and I didn't want to wake him. I'm going to try again today." Heather's bullet had grazed Harper's side, and it was a miracle she hadn't hit any organs.

"Speak of the devil," Granny said. A light knock came

against the back door of the apartment and I jumped up a little too eagerly, warranting a single eyebrow raise from my dad.

"What? He risked his life for me. The least I can do is not keep him standing out there with a recent bullet wound," I said.

"Mmhmm." My dad stood. "I'll give you some privacy. I could use a nap anyway," he said.

I waited for my dad to make it halfway up the staircase before I rushed to open the back door. Harper stood on the small wooden porch, a smile already plastered on his face.

"Harper!" I couldn't hide my excitement and threw my arms around him. "I'm so glad you're okay!"

He chuckled but I felt him wince in pain.

"Sorry!" I pulled back.

"It's okay. Just a little scrape really. I'll be fine."

"I was going to come see you today. I didn't think they'd release you from the hospital yet." I crossed my arms over my chest, slightly embarrassed about how excited I'd been to see him.

"Like I said, just a little scrape. No reason to stay there any longer than I need to. Besides, I wanted to come check on you."

"Check on *me*? I'm not the one who got shot."

"While you do have a point there, you still went through something pretty traumatic. Someone did try to kill you. I just wanted to make sure you're okay."

"I will be." I nodded, and for the first time I believed it.

"I noticed the bookstore is closed today," he commented.

"Yeah, I'm all out of employees, I'm afraid. It hasn't been high on my priority list the last two days either. Peaches suggested I have Astra and Electra come help out since they're only working at the café part-time anyway. And Dorothy and Eve both offered to help out too. So we'll be back in business tomorrow."

"That's great." He smiled. "Well, I wanted to stop by and see you, but I also thought you might want to know that we wrapped up the murder investigations."

"What about Heather? Chief Carver never even questioned me that night and he hasn't been by since."

"Chief Carver spoke with both myself and the rest of the ladies that were here. The case is closed and no further investigation is necessary."

"But how? I mean, she flew out a window. That's pretty suspicious, isn't it?"

"Dru, Chief Carver has been around for a long time, remember? You don't get to be Police Chief in this town without knowing most of the people around here. And their secrets."

"Wait, Chief Carver knows I'm a witch?" I asked.

Harper nodded. "I guess he found out about all of you back when your mom died. Or—well, when everything went down with your mom and the witch hunter."

"I guess I shouldn't be surprised. I feel like everyone knows more about my life than I do."

"You're learning, though," he encouraged.

"I have a question I've been meaning to ask you. How did you know Heather was allergic to bees?" I asked.

Harper laughed. "I didn't. I was just trying to shift into something small enough to escape the ropes and it was the first thing that came to mind. I figured while I was in that form I might as well sting her. It was just dumb luck, really."

I could feel my heart thudding in my chest as I worked up the courage to say what I needed to. "Listen, I owe you an apology. I know sorry doesn't even come close to being enough, but—"

He held up his hand. "No need to apologize."

"Harper, I hit you over the head with a vase and tied you up. I nearly got you killed. I *definitely* need to apologize," I argued.

He shook his head. "No, you don't. What you did made perfect sense given the circumstances. You had no idea I was your Guardian and someone that you trusted told you I was the bad guy. You don't need to apologize for doing what you needed to do to protect yourself. As for nearly getting killed, well, that's what I signed up for. My life for yours."

I knew he meant because he was supposed to protect me, but there was something in his eyes that made my heart leap in my chest.

"Well, I've got to get down to the station and finish up some reports," he said, but he didn't move. His eyes searched mine. "Uh, by the way, I still owe you a meal." His voice had taken on a husky tone.

"A meal?"

"Yeah, when you first got here, I told you I'd take you to try the best spots in town, remember?"

"I do. That would be great." My dad's words about not getting too close to your Guardian unexpectedly flooded my brain, "I'm glad to have you as a friend," I added reluctantly.

"Yup. A friend." Harper's voice faltered just a bit. "Well, I'll see you around." He offered me his best smile, but I read the disappointment in his eyes.

I waited until he reached the bottom of the outside steps and started off down the sidewalk before I closed the door and moved over to the window to watch him. I felt Granny at my side.

"Is there like an anti-love spell?" I asked.

"Oh, I'm sure your personality will do the trick just fine."

"Ma!" my mom scolded.

219

"Very funny, Granny. But I meant one that I could use on myself." I sighed.

She hesitated for a moment before she spoke. "None that I've seen actually work. If two people are destined to be together, no amount of magic can keep them apart. Just ask your mother."

THANK YOU

*T*hank you so much for reading! The Blackwood Bay Witches mystery series is an ongoing series. You can see a full list of books by the author on the following page.

One final note … if you'd like to be notified of new releases, giveaways, and special deals, you can sign up for my newsletter on my website at www.mistybane.com. Not an email person? You can also keep track of my new releases by following me:

On Facebook

On Bookbub

On Amazon

Newsletter Sign Up

ABOUT THE AUTHOR

Misty Bane is a Pacific Northwest native currently living somewhere between the mountains and the beach with her husband, three children, and golden retriever, Lou. She often fantasizes about living in a world where she could clean the house and whip up a four-course meal with just a twirl of her finger.

Keep up with Misty by following her on social media. To be notified of new releases and special discounts, join her newsletter list. She has a strict anti-spam policy and you will never receive anything you didn't sign up for.

You can also join her Facebook Reader Group.

Or Email: misty@mistybane.com

Made in the USA
Monee, IL
27 March 2021